The Love of His Life?

"Peter!" Nancy cried over the noise of the party. "It feels like I haven't seen you in weeks."

Peter smiled crookedly. "But we just saw each other at your office when I stopped by to say thanks for our terrific date last week. Remember?" Since then he'd wanted to call her every day, but he hadn't. He had to have time to think.

"You haven't been avoiding me, have you?" Nancy asked jokingly. "I was wondering about our second date, the one you mentioned the other day."

Peter's eyes slid away guiltily. He remembered the sweet smell of the perfume she'd been wearing and the brief, petal-like touch of her hand on the side of his face. And then the thought that maybe things were going a little too quickly. "I—I'd love to, but I'm kind of swamped right now," he said unconvincingly.

"Sure. Whatever." Nancy shrugged. Her eyes were filled with questions, but all she said was, "Just wondering. See you around."

As Nancy weaved back into the crowd, a realization hit Peter like a slap across the face: Nancy was the one girl who was right for him.

NANCY DREW ON CAMPUS™

Available from ARCHWAY Paperbacks

Nancy Drew
on campus™ #4

Tell Me
the Truth

Carolyn Keene

AN ARCHWAY PAPERBACK
Published by POCKET BOOKS
New York London Toronto Sydney Tokyo Singapore

AN ARCHWAY PAPERBACK *Original*

An Archway Paperback published by
POCKET BOOKS, a division of Simon & Schuster Inc.
1230 Avenue of the Americas, New York, NY 10020

Copyright © 1995 by Simon & Schuster Inc.
Produced by Mega-Books, Inc.

ISBN: 0-671-52745-2

First Archway Paperback printing December 1995

10 9 8 7 6 5 4 3 2 1

NANCY DREW, AN ARCHWAY PAPERBACK and colophon
are registered trademarks of Simon & Schuster Inc.

NANCY DREW ON CAMPUS is a trademark of
Simon & Schuster Inc.

Cover photos by Pat Hill Studio

Printed in the U.S.A.

IL 8+

Tell Me
the Truth

CHAPTER 1

'Casey Fontaine's amazing career, which began in a high school production of *Grease!*, will go back to the future this month when the TV star turned college student appears in Wilder's own production of the popular musical.'

"I've read this article so many times, I can't tell if it's any good," Nancy Drew murmured as she finished reading aloud a section from her celebrity profile of her suitemate and glamorous ex-TV star, Casey Fontaine. She leaned back in the chair in her tiny cubicle at the *Wilder Times* and squinted at the computer screen in the early morning sunlight.

"Sounds good to me," an unidentified voice said from somewhere in the deserted office.

Nancy whirled around. A dozen blank computer screens stared back—but no people.

"You definitely need more sleep," Nancy told

herself, and slumped over her desk. "You're starting to hear things—"

"I didn't think you were the kind of girl who talked to herself," the voice responded.

"I'm not," Nancy replied uncertainly, scanning the room.

Her eyes settled on a desk in the far corner. Jake Collins's desk. Jake Collins: junior hot shot and star reporter. One day that desk would be hers, she had decided. Out of the corner of her eye she saw a mussed tangle of wavy brown hair rise from behind a wall of papers and pizza boxes stacked on the desk. Then a pair of black cowboy boots stepped around the desk and Jake Collins came into the light.

Nancy had seen Jake at editorial meetings, but they weren't friends. In fact, they hadn't even had a conversation since she joined the paper. He was one of those guys that freshman girls like her could never talk to, or even get near.

She admired his hard-boiled, investigative articles, but was intimidated by his signature steel-tipped cowboy boots and his gorgeous eyes: warm brown, bottomless, like pieces of glass held up to the light.

Supposedly, he was really funny. To Nancy, though, he seemed deadly serious, always at his computer, churning out feature after feature—the embodiment of a dedicated reporter.

Nancy couldn't stop herself from smiling at the unruly mess atop Jake's head. "Nice hair."

Jake squinted at her with mock venom as he pushed a hand back through his tangles.

"Have you been here *all* night?" she asked.

Jake shrugged. "I had a deadline for Gail, and I accidentally fell asleep. It happens every now and then. Get used to it." He nodded toward Nancy's computer. "I can't wait to see your piece on Casey Fontaine," he said. "It sounds good." He leaned down and read from the computer screen:

" 'I want everyone to know that I am Casey Fontaine and not my character on *The President's Daughter*, Ginger Porter,' Fontaine said. 'Ginger's a kid. I'm tired of playing a kid. I'm a college woman now.' "

"Great quote," Jake said admiringly.

"Really?" Nancy replied, astonished by Jake's compliment. He had the reputation of being a brutal critic of everyone else's writing.

"Thanks," she said hesitantly. "I want to get the story just right to make some points with Gail," Nancy said, referring to the paper's editor-in-chief, Gail Gardeski.

Jake nodded. "I heard all about Casey's crazy little stalker friend—sounds like something straight out of a movie."

Nancy nodded. "It was."

When Casey moved into Nancy's suite, Suite 301, she hadn't only brought her fame and suitcases. She'd also brought along the obsessions of a love-crazed high school friend who sent her scary letters and eventually tried to kidnap her.

Luckily, Nancy and some of the other girls in the suite had stopped him.

Just then a light came into Jake's eyes, as if he'd just thought of something. "Hey, why don't you look at this issue's page-one story and tell me what you think. Hot off the press. You'll be the first to read it."

Nancy swallowed hard. "You want to know what *I* think?"

"Why not?" Jake said easily. He disappeared behind the papers and pizza boxes and surfaced with a fresh newspaper. Placing it in Nancy's outstretched hands, he looked into her eyes and held her gaze for a second with his own. "You're a really good writer."

Nancy found Jake's eyes beautiful and magnetic, with a determined expression.

Nancy dropped her gaze. "Do you think so? But how can you know?" she said, doubt in her voice. "I've only done a couple stories."

"Well"—Jake smiled—"that bit about Casey Fontaine's hair? That was totally killer!"

They looked at each other for a second, then both erupted in nervous laughter.

"Besides," Jake explained, "only a good writer would bother to get in here early on a Monday morning. . . ."

That made Nancy smile. *Somebody* appreciated her efforts. "Flattery will get you everywhere," she said, and concentrated on the paper. The headline stretched across the top: "Jefferson

College Hackers Crack Computer Codes and Steal Exams."

As Nancy pored over the article, she couldn't believe what she was reading. A small group of computer geeks at nearby Jefferson College had turned out to be part of a ring of sophisticated high-tech burglars. These burglars had developed ingenious computer programs to break into professors' private files. For the right price, they would steal any exam or change a grade. They were caught only when the FBI came in and set up a sting operation. The college administration had managed to cover up the scandal to save face, but Jake found an anonymous source who told all. The story had controversy written all over it, and the writing was snappy and tight.

"This is amazing," Nancy said, looking up from the paper. Jake was kneeling, reading along with her. "I mean, it's excellent."

"Think so?" he asked as if he could hardly believe it.

For a second Nancy saw anxiety in Jake's eyes.

"Really," Nancy assured him. "How did you get all that information?"

Jake smiled wryly and patted the notebook he always carried in his back pocket. "First lesson in journalism. Never reveal your sources."

Glancing back at the paper, Nancy saw Jake Collins's byline below the headline, and felt a flash of envy. She was eager to break stories like this herself.

"Your time will come," Jake said as though he'd read Nancy's mind.

Nancy smiled politely. "Thanks, but—"

"No, I mean it. I have a good feeling about you." He was staring at her as though trying to size her up. Then he unsuccessfully swallowed a yawn. "Let's get a cup of coffee at Java Joe's sometime and talk shop. But . . . hey, what time is it, anyway?"

"Seven o'clock," Nancy answered him.

"Seven," Jake repeated spacily. "Better catch a cold shower. I have a geology exam in two hours."

As he reached the door, he turned around. "By the way, I wasn't kidding about your writing. You may be a first-semester freshman, but I think you have the makings of a journalist."

Before Nancy could say anything, Jake was gone. The door closed on the morning light, and Nancy was alone again.

Her mind was racing. Why was Jake suddenly paying attention to her? Before this morning, he acted as if he didn't know she was alive.

But why question a good thing? Nancy chided herself. He's a lot nicer than you thought. And he obviously wants to help. Relax. Who are you to turn him down?

"Will, cut it out!" George Fayne scolded her boyfriend, Will Blackfeather, with a mock frown. "I can't believe you. I have my first big exam in

6

western civ, and you promised me you'd study, too."

"I *am* studying," Will whispered with a sly grin. "I'm studying you!"

George tried a mean glare but gave up. It was hopeless. No, not hopeless, George thought with a sigh—pathetic. "You're dangerous," she whispered, leaning her head of wavy brown hair against Will's muscular chest. She closed her eyes, and all thoughts of her upcoming western civ exam vanished. Even here in the library, where they'd both taken a vow of silence and concentration, they couldn't keep their attention focused on their books.

The truth was, George couldn't be happier. The past few weeks since she met Will, she'd been totally intoxicated with love. She hadn't kept up with her homework, and she hadn't spent much time with her old friends, Nancy and Bess Marvin. She felt like a planet orbiting the sun— and that was tall, dark, and handsome Will Blackfeather.

Now she was in serious trouble, though. Twenty-four hours and counting until her exam. And how much studying had she done? Zero. Zilch. Zippo.

Earth to George Fayne, a little voice warned her.

George's eyes popped open. She took a playful swipe at Will's hand, which had been busy stroking her knee. She straightened up and narrowed her eyes.

"Tell me the truth, Will, do you want me to fail this exam?" she asked.

"Negative," Will replied tightly.

Up and down the row of study carrels, people cleared their throats. George's cheeks turned bright pink.

Rolling his eyes, Will lowered his voice to a whisper. "But I thought you were a genius."

"I *am* a genius." George smiled. "But even geniuses need to nurture their superior minds."

George and Will collapsed in silly giggles, which stopped only when their foreheads collided.

Suddenly a paper airplane streaked overhead and plunked Will in the ear. Barely containing her laughter, George unfolded it. It was a note. It said, simply: "Go away! I need to study!"

Scowling, Will stood and started to crane his neck down the line of carrels, but George snatched at his belt and tugged him back down.

"They're right," George whispered, taking Will by the hand. "Listen, next week this exam will be over—and then it's just us."

"Just you and me?" Will asked as if he'd forgotten about their big camping trip. Just that day they'd reserved their tent site with the Park Service.

"Just you, me, the stars—and the mosquitoes. In Andy's tent."

Will's roommate, Andy Rodriguez, had promised them his camping gear. Their entire trip hinged on it.

"You know, I haven't seen Andy in days. He's been spending most of his time at the computer lab in Graves Hall, working on some project. The only way I know he's been in the room is whether his toothbrush has moved, or his mountain of dirty laundry has grown."

"You don't think he'd forget he's going to lend us his stuff?" George asked, frowning. "He knows how important this trip is to us, doesn't he?"

Will shrugged. "He's totally into this computer thing. But that's my problem. I'll get us that tent. In the meantime—"

"Right," George said, suddenly earnest. "What I was saying was that this week—"

Will pressed a finger against her lips. "You're not the only one with an exam around here. I'll leave you alone under one condition only."

"Anything." George smiled up at him.

"That after you finish studying, you'll come to my apartment—for some biology review."

"But I'm not taking bio," George said, playing dumb.

"Not yet." Will smiled lovingly.

"Please, please, *please* let Nancy's suite be empty," Bess Marvin prayed as the elevator doors opened on the third floor of Thayer Hall.

As she checked her appearance in the metal doors, she rolled her eyes with a grimace. There was nothing wrong with her: blue eyes sparkling, blond hair shimmering, her purple leotard top flattering her curves under her jacket. Bess looked great and knew it. All the glances from guys around campus hadn't escaped her notice.

It was the textbook balancing on her head that threw off her appearance. Carrying the book was chore-of-the-day for Kappa's freshman pledges. From morning till night, wherever Bess went, the book went with her. She had to walk pole straight so the book wouldn't slide off: back taut, neck stiff—like a whiplash victim. Everywhere she went, she felt a trail of laughter. She'd blushed so often, her face felt sunburned.

"Why am I doing this?" Bess wondered out loud, peering uneasily around her. She was far enough from the Kappa house that it was unlikely a Kappa would catch her without the book, but she couldn't be too careful. Bess remembered what Soozie Beckerman, Kappa upperclassman and official taskmaster, had told her. These "little chores" reduced all pledges to the same lowly status, bonding them in sisterhood. "Consider the chores as tokens of your commitment," Soozie had told them. "The Big Test is yet to come. If you want to be a Kappa badly enough, you'll do anything."

"Including look like a total loser in front of the whole university," Bess muttered.

Before she got the door to Nancy's suite open, Bess knew her prayers hadn't been answered. The suite was a nightmare of frenetic activity. Girls were lounging on the couch, running in and out of the bathroom, packing and unpacking bookbags. As Bess stepped inside, the lounge fell silent for a beat or two before filling with laughter.

"That, um, really suits you, Bess," Stephanie Keats drawled. "Is that the latest fall fashion? Or are we just working on our posture?"

Of course Stephanie was looking her usual slinky, mysterious self in well-worn jeans and a skimpy black halter top, her hair artfully tousled, her mouth enticing and menacing in bloodred lipstick.

"Give her a break," Reva Ross said, lifting the book off Bess's head. Reva's head was wrapped swamilike in a towel. Her graceful, burnished arms were still wet from a shower. "You don't have to do any stupid pledge stuff in here. We're already sisters."

Stephanie rolled her eyes. "Too many sisters is more like it," she wisecracked.

"Thanks, Reva," Bess said, ignoring Stephanie's remark. She took back the book and placed it carefully on her head. "But I'd better keep this thing on. You never know," she said, staring directly at Stephanie. "They said they have spies everywhere—"

Everyone's eyes shifted toward Stephanie.

Stephanie raised her arms in mock surrender. "Don't look at me."

"What's so funny?" Bess heard a familiar voice call from down the hall. By the time Nancy reached the lounge, she was laughing in spurts.

"Oh, Bess, there's a book on your head," Nancy said, controlling her laughter for a bit.

"Okay, okay," Bess said, exasperated. "Why doesn't everybody just get it over with and laugh really hard. Ha, ha."

"Sensitive, aren't we?" Stephanie quipped, strolling off toward her room.

"Gotta run, Nance," Nancy's roommate Kara Verbeck said as she flew past. When she noticed Bess, she stopped dead in her tracks and whirled around, giggling. "It's a good thing Pi Phi hasn't made me do anything that silly." Then she was gone.

"Don't worry, Bess," Reva said, catching the door with her toe. "Kara's not exactly a test for what's silly. But no rest for the weary. I have to get to the computer lab."

As Bess followed Nancy back toward her room, she was thinking that the one person she wanted to avoid was Casey Fontaine. Casey was a celebrity, but everyone was cool about her being famous except for Bess's future Kappa sisters. The Kappas wanted Casey to pledge their sorority. Since Bess saw Casey both in Nancy's suite and at rehearsals for *Grease!*, the Kappas had given Bess the all-important assignment of recruiting Casey.

It didn't matter to them that Casey hadn't shown up at a single rush party or indicated in any way that she wanted to be a Kappa. If Bess succeeded, she'd be a hero; if she failed, her name would be mud—especially with Soozie Beckerman.

"This book thing's the least of it," Bess complained, following Nancy into her room. "Soozie had me clean her bathroom floor with a toothbrush last night."

"Hey, Nance?" someone asked from the doorway. "Can I borrow your calculator? Mine's—"

Bess winced. She'd know that voice anywhere—after all, it was world famous. And worse, it was already laughing at her. "Hi, Casey," Bess whispered, her face turning from pink to tomato red.

"Uh, hi, Bess?" Casey said, and snickered.

Out of the corner of her eye, Bess could see the adorable Casey Fontaine taking her in. Tall, willowy, with short flame red hair and a cover girl's creamy complexion, Casey would have been the envy of every girl at Wilder, if she wasn't so generous and nice. The fact was, she was incredibly cool. But some of the Kappas cared only that she was famous.

"What are you guys up to today?" Casey asked as Nancy handed the actress her calculator. Bess noticed that Casey couldn't keep her eyes off Bess's head.

"Power studying," Nancy replied. "Whopper western civ exam for me tomorrow."

"All right. Well, I'm library bound!" Casey said, raising her clenched fist with mock enthusiasm. Starting to leave, she stopped short and turned to Bess. "You're pretty red. Getting too much sun there, Marvin? Careful, or you'll wrinkle early." Then she was gone.

Bess sat heavily on Nancy's bed, the book clattering to the floor. "Great," she said. "There's no way Casey will join Kappa now—not after seeing all the stupid pledge stuff I have to do. I'm a total failure."

"Well, that book thing's not exactly a brilliant concept," Nancy pointed out. "Whose idea was it, anyway?"

"Soozie Beckerman's," Bess mumbled.

"Why aren't I surprised?" Nancy tossed off.

Bess dumped out her knapsack on Nancy's bed. Out poured a cascade of assorted papers, books, pens, pennies, and bubble gum wrappers. She sifted through the heap for her biology notes.

"It's really remarkable how much more organized college has made you." Nancy laughed.

"I know, I know, I'm a total slob," Bess said with a sigh. "But I can't worry about that now. I'm doing miserably in all my classes and really need to pass my new exams to bring my grades up."

"You've just got to make time to study, Bess," Nancy said.

"Well, I have no idea how you get *any* studying done around here," Bess replied. "This place is a total zoo."

"If you think this is crazy, just wait until you're living in the Kappa house next year. I hear sleep is rare."

Bess dropped her notes and fell back on Nancy's bed with a moan. "What good is joining a sorority if I'm just going to flunk out?" she wondered out loud.

"Knock, knock." Ginny Yuen, another of Nancy's suitemates, strolled in. She looked warily at Bess's stuff spread all over the bed.

"Approach at your own risk," Bess groaned.

"You're studying for Professor Ross's biology class," Ginny observed, picking up a page of notes. "I do work-study for him."

Bess sat up. "You work for Ross?"

"Just research and some grading."

"My roommate works for him, too," Bess said.

"You actually *live* with Leslie King?" Ginny asked, amazed.

"I wouldn't say I live *with* Leslie," Bess said sarcastically, thinking of the obsessively neat girl who slept across the room from her every night. "Live *under* her is more like it."

Ginny glanced at the notes she held in her hand. "That's going to be one hard test," Ginny warned.

Bess threw up her hands. "Great! Excellent! I don't have a prayer."

"Sure you do," Nancy said, assuring her friend.

Ginny lit up the room with a wide smile. "I've been studying pretty hard for the test," she said. "And I know that stuff really well. Maybe I can help you."

"Honestly?" Bess said, excited.

"I'm already tutoring one or two other people," Ginny said. "Let's give it a try now."

* * *

She and Bess sat side by side with Bess's notes. Half an hour later Bess was nodding and acting a lot less glum. "I'm getting it!" she exclaimed. "Wow, Ginny, you're a great teacher."

Ginny shrugged modestly. "Any time."

"Really?" Bess wondered.

"Sure. We could meet at Java Joe's or somewhere and go over your notes. Whatever. I don't mind."

"What about next week? Same time?"

"Sounds good," Ginny smiled.

"And now, maybe, I won't flunk tomorrow's bio test!" Bess said.

"Oh my gosh!" Ginny said suddenly, hopping to her feet. "Nancy, what time is it?"

Nancy looked at her watch. "Five after eleven."

"Already five minutes late for a meeting with Ross! He hates that! I better get going. See ya."

As Ginny blew out the door, Bess leaned back against Nancy's pillows, her bio notes stacked neatly in her lap, a smug expression on her face. She started to whistle.

"Happy now?" Nancy said, grinning at her friend.

"Things sure are looking up!" Bess said happily.

In an apartment building on the far side of campus, he sat before his high-tech computer console. A single piece of paper, labeled Introduction to Biology, Professor Ross, was tacked to the wall. It listed the class's exam and lab schedule. That morning's *Wilder Times* was spread across his lap, the article about the computer cheating scandal marked and underlined and doodled on.

"Thank you, Jake Collins," he murmured, nervously drumming his fingers as he impatiently eyed the screen.

"Come on," he prodded the computer. "Give it to me; give it to me."

Finally the screen filled with the student list for Ross's class.

"Thank you," he said.

Next to each student's name were grades from labs and quizzes. As his eye flew to each F and D, he mentally noted the students who were already in danger of failing the class.

"Okay, Professor Ross," he said, quickly typing in a new series of commands. "You think you're going to humiliate more people, fail them, ruin their futures? You think you're going to ignore your students' requests for help? Not a chance. I'm going to make sure of it."

CHAPTER 2

"Hey, you slacker!" Reva said as she elbowed Andy Rodriguez in the shoulder. "Stop crowding me."

"Who're you calling a slacker?" Andy kidded back, shooting at an elbow, too. *"You're* crowding *me!"*

Reva raised her head as she heard the muffled sound of the campus clock chime three o'clock. Even though the clock tower was right outside, it sounded miles away. She and Andy were underground, huddled side by side in front of a computer monitor in the labyrinthine computer lab underneath Graves Hall. The past week they had been hired by the university to put together a student guide for the Internet, the international computer network.

Their most important task was to make the guide easy to understand, since a lot of students were still intimidated by computers. The guide had to explain how the Internet could be used, by first showing how it was simply a network of people around the world, all plugged into a single "library" of information. Students could "talk" to students at other colleges on their computers; read books and magazines on-line; exchange information with other readers; and do research.

Just as there were different sections in a library for literature and history and music, there were different "sections" on the Internet. The only difference was that instead of going to a library building, students would connect to it through telephone lines and the words would appear on computer screens.

The more Reva learned about the Internet, the more amazing it became to her. She realized that Wilder students had an entire world of information at their fingertips. All they needed was a computer and a phone line—and a little help from Andy and her!

"You know how long we've been down here?" she asked, finally leaning back from the humming monitor and rubbing her eyes. Reva pushed aside the dozen or so candy wrappers that had accumulated around them. "Six hours straight! My brain is oatmeal."

"Call 911, we're losing brain cells fast!" Andy said with mock urgency. He stretched his legs. "I've been seeing double for about an hour now. I don't even know which screen to read."

"That's the problem with working underground," Reva said. "You lose track of time, and your brain turns to mush." Then she moaned and grabbed her stomach. "I feel like I've eaten a million candy bars."

"Um, I believe it was only ten," Andy said.

"Ten?" Reva asked in disbelief. "That's disgusting."

Andy nodded. "I agree."

"I don't even remember eating them," Reva said.

Andy shook his head. "Now, *that's* disgusting." He rubbed the back of his neck. "Boy, I'm totally stiff."

"Turn around," Reva commanded.

Andy gave her an inquiring look.

"Obey first, ask later," Reva said with a smile.

Shrugging, Andy turned his back to her. Reva grabbed his shoulders in her hands and began to knead them slowly.

"Ooh, that's good," Andy groaned, his head falling forward. "Higher, harder— Ouch! Not so hard!"

"Sorry." Reva chuckled and cuffed Andy on the side of the head. Even though they kidded around like buddies, Reva couldn't deny that she liked the feel of Andy's muscular shoulders in her hands.

Actually, when Reva first met Andy, she wasn't sure they'd get along. He knew more about computers than she did, but she was the better writer. He didn't talk much, which made it tough to exchange ideas about the best way to phrase things in the guide. But they were stuck together—the university had hired them both.

Over the last few days, Reva swore she saw Andy staring at her reflection in the computer screen. When she glanced back, his eyes would slip away. She couldn't deny that he was extremely handsome, with dark hair, black, mysterious eyes, and a delicately chiseled face. She'd started to feel something growing between them, like an energy field. She felt it whenever they sat down to get to work.

With Andy, it wasn't work, she thought, as she leaned forward far enough to feel the heat from the back of his neck. It was fun. But was it more?

Crossing her long, slim legs, Leslie King smiled contentedly as Ginny Yuen burst through Professor Ross's door, out of breath.

"I'm really sorry," Ginny panted, taking the big leather chair next to Leslie's across from his desk.

Professor Ross cleared his throat and threw Ginny a withering look. "I was just telling Miss King that this year's freshman class seems more intelligent than past years' classes, but not necessarily more responsible."

Serves her right, Leslie thought to herself.

The fact was, Leslie's jealousy toward Ginny had been building ever since they'd wound up sharing the same work-study job. Professor Ross seemed to give Ginny more responsibility. Ginny would proofread the professor's papers while Leslie would straighten up his desk. While Ginny was researching some new technology in biomedical engineering, Leslie was filling out order forms for laboratory equipment, which required all the skill of an orangutan.

Leslie was seething. After all, *she* was the one who needed the excellent recommendation from Professor Ross on her future medical school applications. Leslie was under incredible pressure from a whole family of prestigious doctors.

"So, Miss King, what do you think of this cheating scandal, the one reported in today's *Times*?" Ross asked.

Leslie squirmed in her seat. "Cheating scandal?"

"This morning's paper. You mean to tell me you don't keep up with your own school paper?" he accused.

"I—I haven't had a chance to—" Leslie stammered.

"Well, I think it's just awful," Ginny chimed in earnestly. She looked composed and beautiful, with her long, straight black hair and huge, expressive eyes. Leslie rolled her eyes. It was enough to make her want to barf.

Ginny met the professor's forthright gaze exactly halfway across the desk. "It's amazing that someone would spend their college education learning how to cheat instead of learning how to learn," she added reasonably.

"Quite right," Ross agreed. "In fact, I've been

predicting something like this for years. Computers used to be privileged equipment, but now they're as common as toys. Again and again I've pushed the administration for an honor code at this university—one something like those at the military academies. No second chances is my philosophy. One mistake and you're out."

"Great idea!" Leslie blurted out, more loudly than she'd intended.

Ross looked annoyed at Leslie's outburst, then returned his attention to Ginny. "In fact," he went on, "just last week, I began to research ways to protect my exams from the likes of the Jefferson College plunderers. I understand that there are ways to hide documents on my computer and then translate them into secret code—"

"I've heard something about that, too." Ginny nodded. "Encryption code, I think it's called."

"Exactly, Miss Yuen," Ross said. "I found a simple program that even I can understand."

Ginny leaned forward, nodding intently. She seemed to understand everything Ross was saying. Leslie leaned forward, too. The problem was, Leslie had used computers primarily to write papers, but she wasn't an expert. She was like almost everyone else: amazed by what computers did while not totally understanding *how* they did it. But Ginny seemed to know what was going on inside them.

Nodding and leaning forward an inch more than Ginny, as if it were a race down to the wire, Leslie faked complete understanding.

"I see what you mean." Ginny nodded with real comprehension.

"Y–yes," Leslie agreed, casting Ginny a sidelong glance.

"Really? So what is your opinion, Miss King?" Professor Ross asked. "What should I do with my computer files?"

Leslie opened her mouth to speak but paused as she searched for an answer.

"I bet what you're doing is good enough," Ginny broke in. "If you protect your files with a password, you'd be extra safe by using encryption to make your exams unreadable—except by anyone who has the encryption program."

Ross flashed Ginny a warm smile. "You seem to know a great deal about this."

Ginny blushed. "Not really," she said.

Leslie leaned back dejectedly, keeping Ginny in her peripheral vision. She needed to steal back Ross's attention.

Ginny has to have some weakness, she thought.

Andy slumped forward, as if Reva's back rub had put him to sleep. Reva leaned forward to check, and she was surprised to find Andy's eyes wide open, staring distractedly at the floor, as if deep in thought.

"Earth to Andy," Reva whispered.

"When do you think the university is going to pay us?" Andy asked out of the blue.

Reva shrugged. "I haven't thought about it."

"They're already a week late," Andy said.

"It's not that much anyway. Besides, I'd do this even if we weren't getting paid."

"Not me."

"If you want you can have my half when we get it," Reva offered.

She felt Andy stiffen, then relax again. "I don't need it *that* badly."

She heard footsteps behind them. "Fellow cave dwellers, unite!" a cheerful voice announced.

"Hi, Stuart," Reva said.

"Just in time for the party, I see," Stuart said. A big, jovial sophomore with thinning sandy hair and a slouch, Stuart O'Brien had volunteered to help them on the Internet project, even though he'd said he didn't know much about computers. But he turned out to be nice to have around: he caught on fast, he was very funny, he didn't cost anything, and three heads were better than two—so why not?

Catching sight of that day's *Wilder Times* in Reva's book bag, Stuart pulled up a chair and sat between them. "Hey, can you believe that cheating story? I'm just catching onto this computer stuff, but I can already see it would have taken a real wizard to do what they did."

"It's not that difficult," Andy remarked.

Stuart paused. "Oh, really?" he said. "Maybe we should keep an eye on you, huh?" He gave Andy a poke in the ribs. Andy smiled weakly.

"During my wild years in junior high," Stuart went on, "I remember one time when there was this whammo test in earth science. I wrote all my

notes in teensy handwriting inside my forearm."
Stuart checked out the reactions of his audience.

"Only problem was," he continued, "it was the
end of the year, and hot! I wore a long-sleeved
shirt to hide my notes. But when I walked into
class, the teacher took one look at my arm and
dragged me off to the principal. I had bled blue
ink right through my shirt!"

Reva, laughing, rolled her eyes. "Some artist."

"Yeah," Stuart said good-naturedly.

"I have this friend—" Andy said mysteriously.
"Well, a friend of a friend really. He's been a
computer hacker for a long time—his hero was
that guy who broke into the computers of the
national defense and set off the launch codes."

"He did that?" Reva whistled. "Really?"

Andy nodded. "He could break into any college file he wanted, change a grade, look at upcoming exams."

"That's awful," Reva said.

Stuart and Andy only shrugged.

Reva looked from one to the other. "Isn't it?"

"I guess," Andy said as if he didn't believe
it was.

Reva threw him a quick, inquiring glance.

"There are huge bucks to be made selling computer information," Stuart continued. "There are
top secret files all over the place. And if you
know what you're doing, you can break into
anything."

"I thought you didn't know much about computers," Reva said.

"I don't," Stuart replied matter-of-factly. "I just read about it. It's in all the newspapers. Look at today's *Wilder Times*."

"He's right," Andy said distractedly. "All the how-to information you want, right out in the open."

"Computers can be dangerous," Reva concluded.

"But potentially lucrative," Stuart added.

Reva shot him a disapproving look. "Stuart!"

"I sure could use some money," Andy murmured.

"I don't know what's gotten into you two," Reva said. "And, Andy, what's this thing with money all of a sudden?"

Andy gave Reva a cold, hard look and clammed up.

"Back to work now, boys and girls," Stuart said.

"Okay, guys," Reva said, swiveling around to the computer screen. "Where were we?"

It was late Monday night, and the libraries were filled to capacity. He pictured everyone doubled over the desks in their study carrels, memorizing dates, furiously reading the assignments they'd blown off for the past few weeks. He imagined that familiar look of panic in everyone's eyes.

"Don't worry," he said out loud, looking down at the stack of papers in his hands: printouts of the next day's exam in Professor Ross's biology class. "I'm the high-tech Robin Hood, taking from the so-called geniuses and giving to all struggling students."

He double-checked the list of Ross's students who had the lowest grades. He counted thirty of them. Then he opened a fresh pack of envelopes. "Twenty-nine—thirty."

He looked at his watch and shot out of his chair. "There's just enough time," he said.

"Come on, Ginny, tell us who we're here to see," Casey prodded.

Ginny eyed the pack of them—Nancy, Stephanie, Casey, Reva, Nancy's friend George and George's boyfriend, Will—and grinned slyly. "No way," she refused good-naturedly, opening the door to the Underground and ushering them in.

A dingy, unspectacular cafeteria by day, at night the Underground was transformed into a cutting-edge hangout. The lights were turned down low; the ceiling was edged with white Christmas lights; each table had a candle in a little glass bowl. There was a bar where you could buy sodas and snacks, and beer if you were twenty-one. Mostly seniors and grad students hung out there, their elbows propped up on the edge of the bar.

That night the place was almost packed. The excitement was almost electric.

"Well, what do you think?" Ginny asked eagerly as the group pulled two tables together and gathered around.

"I think it's great," Nancy said enthusiastically, taking in her surroundings. "Definitely has atmosphere."

"It's—okay, I guess," Stephanie admitted reluctantly, lighting up a cigarette. "At least everyone here is fashion conscious." In ten seconds a cloud of smoke had settled over their two tables.

George made a face. "Good thing you're not allowed to smoke," she muttered.

"You come here a lot, Gin?" Casey asked, impressed.

"I guess. I like to listen to the original music. Some of the poems people recite are incredible."

Stephanie snorted. "Come *on*," she whined. *"Poems?"*

"You know, Stephanie—Wordsworth, Robert Frost?" Will tossed off.

"Uh-huh." Stephanie rolled her eyes.

"Green Eggs and Ham? Dr. Seuss?" Nancy offered.

"Well, okay," Stephanie conceded to general laughter. *"Green Eggs and Ham* I *suppose* is cool."

"I'm always amazed at how talented people are," Ginny said earnestly, leaning over the table. "Like last week this total gear-head, who's always whipping around campus on his motorcycle, swaggered through the tables. Then he got up on stage and read a totally beautiful poem about his father. He had the place in tears."

"Boo-hoo," Stephanie mocked her.

"Come on, Steph," Casey said. "We all know you're a softy at heart."

"No way!" Stephanie protested, as if Casey had repeated a vicious rumor.

When are they going to start? Ginny wondered, drumming her fingers on the table, her eyes sweeping the empty little stage. They're going to hate him, I just know it.

"So," Nancy said, grinning at her meaningfully. "Are you going to tell us why we're here, or are we going to have to tickle it out of you?"

Just as Ginny opened her mouth, a smattering of applause rippled through the crowd. Everyone turned toward the stage. Two guys with electric guitars stood front and center, one of them at a mike. Another guy settled behind the drums, a fourth took up a string bass.

The crowd hushed. The guy at the mike cleared his throat. "I'm Ray Johansson," he said in a raspy voice. "And we're the Beat Poets."

"And you're totally gorgeous," Ginny heard Stephanie mutter under her breath.

He *is* gorgeous, Ginny agreed, her eyes sparkling as Ray stomped three times for the band to kick in behind him. The speakers exploded with sound. Ginny was in heaven. Ray had a lean body and black hair. The arm that strummed his guitar was tattooed with an eagle in flight. When Ginny looked at him, the first words that came to mind were *charisma* and *honest*.

Which is exactly what the band's music was like: deep, rough chords, hauntingly poetic lyrics.

30

Ginny smiled as she saw everyone in the little club nodding to the driving beat, totally mesmerized.

"Are these the guys you wanted us to see, Ginny?" Nancy inquired, obviously impressed.

Ginny smiled broadly.

"They're good," Will said to no one in particular.

"What do you think, Casey?" George asked.

Ginny eagerly waited for Casey's answer. Casey had been in show business for years. If anyone would know, she would.

Ginny always thought you could tell what someone was really thinking by their eyes. And if Casey's were any indication, she liked what she heard. "Good," Casey said with the reasonableness of an expert. "Very, very good. *He's* amazing," she added, nodding toward the lead singer.

Ginny's heart leaped as the song came to an end and the Underground erupted in enthusiastic applause. Even Stephanie was smiling—well, more like smirking. And who knew if she even heard the music; she was busy drinking in the sight of Ray Johansson.

Three songs later, the band put down their instruments and took a break. Will volunteered to get a few pitchers of soda and a few bowls of chips. All the talk was about the band. Everyone was grilling Ginny about how she knew them. Stephanie in particular.

"Let me get this straight," she said, shaking her head in disbelief. "You know these guys?"

But Ginny refused to budge. Then Ray Johansson stepped off the stage and twisted his way through the little tables. Everyone was patting him on the back, shaking his hand.

As he headed their way, Stephanie quickly swallowed her mouthful of chips and tugged at her skintight silk blouse. She sat up straight to reveal as much of her slinky body as she could.

"Hey, great sound," Casey called to him.

"Thanks," Ray said humbly, in the same raspy voice. But his eyes were on someone else. He reached out his hand toward Stephanie, who smiled wanly, playing hard to get. But Ray cruised right past her, took Ginny's hand, and kissed her hard on the lips.

"How were we?" Ray asked her, genuinely interested.

"Really tight," she replied lovingly. She cleared her throat and turned Ray toward the table. "Everyone—meet Ray Johansson. Ray—everyone."

"Hi, everyone." Ray blushed, holding up a hand.

"No," Stephanie muttered, staring in utter amazement at Ginny then at Ray and then back to Ginny.

"Well, Ginny," Nancy said, smiling from ear to ear. "I think you've been keeping something from us."

"I'll say," George agreed.

"I wouldn't have kept *him* a secret in a million years," Casey chimed in.

Ginny blushed. She didn't know what to say. It was true she hadn't told anyone about Ray. She was afraid everyone would think she wasn't cool enough to have Ray for a boyfriend. Sexy singers don't go out with nerdy premeds. It just didn't happen.

But it *did* happen, Ginny reminded herself, confident enough now to return her suitemates' winks and nudges.

She and Ray met when he had played solo at the club two weeks ago. He'd bumped into her at the bar between sets. After the show, they sat cross-legged in the grass in the middle of the quad, talking until dawn. As the sun was coming up, he leaned over and kissed her. And now, amazingly, they were starting to fall in love.

"So where does 'Beat' come from in your band's name?" Will asked. "The Beat Generation?"

"The *music* beat," George guessed.

"Actually," Ray said with a shrug, "it's because we practice all night and we're always totally beat in the morning."

"How romantic," Stephanie said in a deadpan.

"Hey, I've got to get back up there," Ray said, as the other band members emerged from behind the curtain in back. "Nice meeting you. 'Bye, Gin." He leaned down and kissed Ginny again, then jogged back onstage.

Reva cleared her throat and pursed her lips. "And how *long* have we been dating Mr. Johansson?" she challenged Ginny, hands on her hips in mock annoyance.

Ginny blushed. "Two weeks," she said with a giggle.

"Two more days and it's over," Stephanie scoffed.

"Ha!" Casey laughed. "You wish, Stephanie."

"Look who's talking!" Stephanie cried.

"Let us not forget"—Casey wagged her finger—"I already have a boyfriend."

"Yeah, a rich and famous one," George added, talking about Charlie Stern, Casey's soulfully handsome ex-costar.

"Don't listen to them, Ginny," Nancy said. "I think you and Ray make a great couple."

Everyone nodded except Stephanie, who was sulking.

Up onstage, Ray cleared his throat and lifted the microphone. "We're back," he said softly to the cheers of the crowd. "I call this one 'Ginny's Song.' "

CHAPTER 3

"Ugh, where *are* you?" Bess groaned, her mouth full of chocolate-chip cookies. Sitting cross-legged on the floor of her room, an island in a sea of books and paper, Bess was digging through her notes for the page Ginny had given her yesterday. Her bio exam was less than an hour away, and she wanted to go over the main points one more time.

Across the room, Leslie sat at her fastidiously arranged desk. She'd made a sort of barricade between her and Bess with notebooks and paper and containers of pens and pencils. White cotton balls stuck out from her ears. For the last hour Bess had noticed her sending over a barrage of annoyed glances. But she wasn't doing anything wrong as far as she could tell. And it was *her* room, too.

"Now, what did I do with that pen?" she asked.

"Behind your ear," Leslie said.

Bess shot a quizzical glance at the cotton balls in Leslie's ears. "Thanks."

Rolling her eyes, Leslie plucked out the cotton balls and fired them at the wastebasket—and missed. "Typical," she groaned. Bending to pick them up, she clipped a can of pens with her elbow and sent them crashing to the floor. Her face reddened with rage. Bess could see her roommate was a land mine just waiting to be tripped.

"Here, let me help," Bess offered, leaning backward to sweep the pens into a manageable pile. Leslie didn't see her coming, and they knocked heads.

"G-get—*away!*" Leslie stammered.

"Sorry," Bess said, rubbing her forehead. She laced her voice with sweetness. "Um, how's your studying going?"

"It's not," Leslie replied icily.

"Don't you have an exam this afternoon?"

Leslie slammed her book closed and shook her head. "Bess, do you see that desk over there?"

Bess eyes followed the direction of Leslie's finger. A desk identical to Leslie's sat totally un-used next to Bess's bed. "Did you ever think of using your desk to study—all the way over *there?*" Leslie asked acidly.

"Yes," Bess replied.

"So?"

The truth was, the desk surface wasn't big enough for Bess. She liked to study in the middle of an expanding puddle of class notes, with everything around her. That way, instead of searching through notebooks and books for something, all she had to do was move her eyes. Wasn't that logical?

Bess shrugged at Leslie's question, and Leslie nodded, as though that was exactly what she expected Bess to say—nothing.

Bess offered her the last cookie. "Want one?"

"I *don't* want a cookie," Leslie snapped. "I want to *study*. And I can't study with all that *noise!*"

Bess glanced around the room. She peered up at the window. It was a gray, cloudy Tuesday morning. Rain was tapping against the glass, running down like tears.

"You mean the rain?" she asked innocently. "I kind of like it. It's soothing—"

"Not the rain, Bess," Leslie cut her off. "I mean the sound of cookie crunching. I can't study with you—here—like *this!*"

Leslie abruptly stood and started shoving books into her knapsack.

Bess blinked up at her, wondering, Am I really *that* annoying? "Where are you going?"

"Anywhere!" Leslie said. "The library, the Laundromat, the train station. Anywhere I don't have to look at that mountain of garbage or listen to the noise of chomping. I can't believe I'm being thrown out of my own room!"

"But I'm not throwing you—"

It was too late. Leslie blew out the door.

Sitting on the floor, Bess listened to the rain. "I'm not any messier than anyone else, am I?" She eyed her side of the room. It was true that Leslie's half was incredibly neat. Bess's half, on the other hand, looked decidedly lived in; clothes hanging out of drawers; bed made but not really; just stuff around—everywhere.

Leaning back against Leslie's empty chair, Bess thought about the roommate questionnaire she'd filled out last spring. It had asked her two dozen questions about her habits and what qualities she'd like in a roommate. Bess had given her answers a lot of thought. Her roommate should be warm, talkative, and generous. They'd sit up all night gossiping and playing cards. They'd go on double dates and laugh about them afterward.

Bess stared dejectedly at Leslie's perfectly made bed: hospital corners, drum tight. In her mind Bess could hear Leslie sniff with displeasure every time she walked in the room. "Did they just throw out my questionnaire, or what?"

In the distance Wilder's clock tower bonged. Bess shot to her feet. The test! I have just enough time to eat breakfast.

"Okay, okay, okay," she chanted, pumping herself up. She paced the room, in her mind going over a checklist of main biological terms.

But the Leslie problem still tugged at her heart. She felt helpless. Okay, she realized, so maybe I'm not the perfect roommate. But does Leslie have to be so mean all the time? I've got to start standing up to her.

"Marvin," she commanded herself, "Shape up! Concentrate! First big test at Wilder." As she left, she couldn't think of a single question to ask herself. She shrugged. "It's probably not important anyway."

"You know this stuff, Ray," Ginny said. "You know you do. It's all up there in your head."

Ray was sitting on his desk in his dorm room, strumming his guitar, while Ginny was sitting in his chair, plowing through his bio notes. "Don't you think *you* should be doing this?" she asked.

"I know who *shouldn't* be doing it," he replied, his fingers walking up the guitar neck like a spider.

"But do you think we covered the section on genetics enough?" she asked, flipping pages.

"Uh-huh," Ray said, bending over to plant a kiss on Ginny's neck.

"What about this stuff about dominant and recessive genes—got that?"

"Got that," Ray echoed, squinting outside at the rain. He mouthed a few stray lyrics he was trying to put together in a new song.

"Ray!" Ginny said, poking him in the ribs. "You have a huge exam in less than an hour."

Ray lay his guitar across his lap and gave Ginny his full attention. "You've really helped me a lot, Gin," he said. "These study sessions have been awesome. It's just that the test is in an hour. I know what I know. Whatever I don't—

well, I figure there's nothing I can do about it now."

Ginny sat back, letting Ray's notes fall to the floor. She didn't know whether to admire his attitude or resent it. Maybe she felt a little of both. She'd been helping him out since they'd met two weeks ago. They both knew he was in trouble with biology. He'd flunked both of the bio pop quizzes, and he'd passed the last lab only with Ginny's help. He did the work she asked him to do, but she knew his heart wasn't in it. All he wanted to do was hold her and play his guitar.

Ray was laughing at her. "You're more nervous about this test than I am." He hummed a few bars of a song he'd been working on. " 'You're so beautiful,' " he sang in a country-rock twang. " 'And I'm so true to . . . to—' " He shook his head. "Wow, it's a lot harder writing a song about someone you love than about someone you don't know."

Ginny blinked up at him. "You're amazing," she said. "I wish I were as laid back as you."

Ray smiled knowingly. "No, you don't. I'm just a hick from the cornfields of Illinois. The only reason I'm here at Wilder is because they felt sorry for me."

"Ray!" Ginny chided him. "You're smart! You earned your scholarship for disadvantaged kids from cities and small towns. You deserved it."

"Because I'm from such a loser place," he said, and laughed bitterly. "You're on scholarship, but your smarts come easily. Look at me. I can barely put two complete sentences together."

"Wrong. You write gorgeous music," Ginny shot back. "You should have seen the look on my friends' faces when you sang last night."

"Well, if they gave points for writing songs, then maybe I'd get somewhere. . . ."

"That's not fair, Ray." Ginny shook her head, straining to keep from getting angry. She hated it when Ray talked like this. He'd told her that night they'd spent sitting in the quad that there was nothing to do in his hometown after high school except get married and have kids. Music had been the only thing that kept him sane. When his Wilder scholarship came along, he became the first person in his family to be admitted to college.

And while it was true that sometimes he seemed more street-smart than book-smart, it was obvious he was a musical genius. He was going to make it big, Ginny was sure of it. He sure wasn't dumb, she thought to herself. He was just different. Different in the best possible way. He was cool, and he was wise.

"It's just a matter of—" Ginny began.

Ray interrupted her, rolling his eyes. "I know, I know. Commitment with a capital *C*. I can be good at whatever I want. You've told me a hundred times."

Ray leaned over to kiss her cheek, and this time she let him. Her eyes closed with pleasure.

I still can't believe how perfect my life is,

Ginny thought, holding Ray's hand. It's almost too good to be true. As much as he believes I'm too good for him, I'm sure he's too good for me.

Strangely, Ray was more comfortable singing in front of a hundred people than talking one on one. But that night they'd sat on the quad, they'd clicked—he a heartthrob guitar player from a Midwest farm, and she a citified premed student whose ancestry traveled back to China. If someone had to pick two people out of a crowd of a thousand to be a couple, the last two they'd pick would be Ginny and Ray. But as different as they were on the outside, Ginny knew, inside they were the same.

Ray's lips were moving up to her ear. "Maybe you could just tell me what's on the test, smarty."

"Ray!" Ginny gave him a playful slap. "I keep telling you I haven't seen it. But even if I had . . ."

Ray held up his hands in mock surrender. "I know, I know. It wouldn't be right."

As Ray picked up his guitar and started to play, Ginny lifted her watch to Ray's face. "Come on, we have to get going."

Ray hopped down from the desk and reached for her.

Ginny tapped her foot. "You're stalling." But she didn't make him chase her. As his strong arms wrapped around her, she surrendered and fell against him.

"I never thought I'd meet someone like you," he said, pressing his lips against her forehead.

Ginny turned her face into Ray's muscular chest. She could hear his heart beating. "Ditto," she said, giving him a hard squeeze.

Ray threw on his leather jacket.

"Hey, can I get one of those, too?" Ginny asked, eyeing his jacket.

Ray laughed. "Why?"

Ginny smiled sheepishly. "Because it's cool."

"But you're cool the way you are," Ray said, his eyes taking her in lovingly.

"Let's go, bio stud," she said.

As they rushed out, they stepped over something lying on the floor outside. "What's that?" Ginny asked. It was a manila envelope with Ray's name on it. Ray kicked it under his door. "I'll get it later," he said. "Probably just someone sending me a song to play. I've been getting a lot of those lately."

"And we thought freshman year was hard," Jake groaned as he sank into one of the couches in the student union lounge. A popular rock song was playing on the loudspeaker. As usual, most of the other couches and chairs were populated with motionless lumps of clothing—students collapsed after all-nighters spent writing papers and studying.

"I heard Ross's bio exam was practically impossible," he said, sinking deeper into the cushioned chair. "And I thought college was supposed to be a vacation."

When Peter Goodwin, his old freshman roommate, didn't reply, Jake opened an eye. "You're supposed to say, 'I need a vacation from my vacation.'"

"What?" Peter said, shaking his head clear.

"Something on your mind?" Jake asked.

Peter shrugged. "Just school stuff."

Jake knew Peter well enough to know when he was stepping around a question and when he was outright lying. Peter was doing both now.

He knew Peter was going through rough times. He'd broken up with Dawn Steiger right after the semester began, and Jake never really understood why. Peter had given him a few reasons, but they were so lame he couldn't even remember them. Jake always thought Dawn was really cool, not to mention gorgeous, a real cover-girl type, tall with long blond hair, a sweet face. Dawn seemed perfect for him. Then whammo— it was over.

Jake leaned over and slapped Peter on the knee. "So what did you think of the story?"

"Story?" Peter asked.

"Hello? Yesterday's *Times*?"

Peter grinned sheepishly. "Great. The best."

"Did you even read it?"

"Sort of," Peter replied unconvincingly.

Jake snarled playfully. "Liar."

"I skimmed it," Peter said.

Jake sat up. "Did you like the way I cornered Jefferson's president into admitting to the cover-up?"

Peter nodded. "Yup. Especially that part."

Jake sipped at his jumbo coffee and sighed. "I met a really interesting girl."

"Uh-huh, no kidding," Peter replied dryly.

"She's really different—"

"Of course she is."

"She works on the newspaper. She's a great writer. But I can tell she's the hard-to-get type."

Peter leaned forward, his brow furrowed. "What about serenading her with a cha-cha band?"

Jake shook his head. "Too hokey. Besides, it brings back bad memories. I tried the cha-cha band bit to ask a girl to my senior prom."

Peter raised his head. "Success or failure?"

Jake gave him a thumbs-down. "She laughed hysterically for about a half hour."

Peter nodded in commiseration. "Okay. How about the candlelit dinner for two in the middle of the quad?"

Jake sighed. "Too clichéd. Anyway, the candles will probably keep blowing out—and then where would I be?"

"I see your point." Peter tapped his forehead. "Candles are out. Is she the outdoorsy type?"

"Good question," Jake said, trying to think. "She seems like it."

"Then what about bungee-jumping for two in that ravine outside town?"

Jake swung his head from side to side. "Too dangerous. Wouldn't want to take the chance that she'd break her beautiful neck." He laughed.

Out of the corner of his eye, Jake noticed a

flash of long, golden hair. "Speaking of beautiful women," he said under his breath, thumbing in that direction.

"Hi, Jake . . . Peter."

Peter raised his head for only second. "Hi, Dawn."

There was a long moment of excruciating silence. Dawn was gazing unhappily at Peter. Peter was looking at Jake, probably hoping Jake would rescue him. Jake, though, wanted no part of it. He never liked other people's romantic battles.

Jake got to his feet. "Oh, would you just look at the time," he said with phony urgency. "I have to get back to my room to study."

"Don't bother," Dawn said sadly. "I won't stay long."

Jake sat. He thought he should make conversation—and quick. "So—Dawn. How were your exams?"

Dawn ignored him. "How are you, Peter?"

"Okay," Peter said with a shrug.

"No, really. You know what I mean."

Peter stiffened and stole a glance in Jake's direction.

"I'm fine," Peter said quickly. "Look, Dawn, maybe we should have a cup of coffee sometime, and have a talk—know what I mean?"

Something odd was going on, Jake was sure of it. He couldn't remember ever seeing his old friend so uncomfortable.

"You know, whatever you want to say to Dawn, you can say in front of me," Jake said.

Dawn looked back and forth between them. "You mean Jake doesn't know?" she asked.

Peter's jaw dropped as he looked up at Dawn in disbelief.

"Know what?" Jake asked, throwing Peter a prodding glance.

"Nothing," Peter growled.

"Come on, guys," Jake complained. "We used to be the Three Musketeers, remember? One for all, and all for one?"

"Not anymore," Peter muttered.

"I have to get back," Dawn said, moving away. "See you around."

"Well, *that* was joyful," Jake joked. Maybe it was the reporter in him, but he'd always hated secrets. Especially serious ones, and especially between friends. He knew Peter and Dawn's breakup had been bad, but he smelled something more going on.

"For what it's worth," Jake said, "I always liked Dawn. I thought you were right for each other. I never understood why you broke up with her. It's just intuition, but I'd say you could have her back."

"I have to go, too," Peter replied abruptly, and strode off in the opposite direction from Dawn.

"Will somebody please tell me what's going on?" Jake asked the empty chair.

What is up? he wondered.

CHAPTER 4

Some quiet celebration," Peter murmured. "I can't even hear myself think."

Peter leaned back in his chair. Even though it was Tuesday night, someone from his second-floor hall in Thayer was throwing a party. By eight o'clock it had transformed itself into something massive, complete with speakers in the hall. Peter tried to do some studying, but people kept knocking on his door, asking if he had the "secret stuff," meaning the illegal keg of beer.

"If you can't beat 'em, join 'em," Peter told his computer before switching it off. He slipped out his door and stood leaning against the wall outside his room. The hall was a sea of bobbing heads. Food and paper cups were everywhere. The only thing missing for Peter was attitude: as much as he tried to get into it, the last thing he felt like doing was partying.

48

He was still depressed about his "conversation" with Jake and Dawn. Peter respected Jake enormously. They'd been through a lot together, and Peter almost always followed his advice. So when Jake said he didn't understand why Peter and Dawn broke up, Peter suddenly had a hard time remembering all the reasons himself.

Maybe I'm crazy, Peter thought as he ducked a flying bag of chips. Out of the corner of his eye, he saw someone who he thought was Dawn. She was Dawn's height, with the same long, silky blond hair. He turned his head, almost feeling that once-familiar leap in his heart. After all, Dawn was gorgeous, intelligent, loving, *and* in love with him. The girl turned. No, it wasn't her.

In his mind he replayed the scene in Dawn's room when he broke up with her. He'd told her they were getting too serious, and he knew he'd never be able to love her the way she loved him.

Then he told her the other reason, the thing that had changed his life, and that would have changed Dawn's, too, if they'd stayed together.

"I don't want to drag you into this," he'd told her.

Dawn had begun to cry. "But I love you," she'd said. "It's not the end of the world. We can deal with it."

"It's my mess," he'd replied firmly. "This is too complicated."

"You're the love of my life," Dawn had said simply, then started to sob.

Jake knows there's something I'm not telling

him, Peter thought. But, it's the one thing in the world I can't tell him. I can barely admit it to myself, but it's probably written all over my face.

Now there was another reason he and Dawn couldn't be together anymore. Peter shook his head, trying to push that thought—and the whole mess—away. But he couldn't. The thought was hanging over him, like a smothering black cloud.

"Peter, over here!"

Peter's thoughts were interrupted by someone waving to him, moving through the crush of kids toward him. Peter's palms grew slick, and he felt the corners of his mouth lift in a smile, as if by themselves. Then he remembered what he was trying so hard to forget.

Instinctively, Peter spun around, trying to slip away unnoticed. It was too late. He was caught.

"Peter!" Nancy cried.

"Hey there," he said, forcing his smile to grow.

"It feels like I haven't seen you in weeks," Nancy said.

Peter smiled crookedly. "But we just saw each other at your office when I stopped by to say thanks for our terrific date last week. Remember? That was only a few days ago."

"But days seem like weeks," Nancy said, reaching out to tickle him. Peter laughed despite himself, trying to twist away. He grabbed Nancy's hands and held them still. He stopped laughing, but Nancy didn't. She looked great: happy and sexy—her reddish blond hair bouncy and alive, her cheeks flushed. She was wearing tight blue jeans and a sweatshirt. Her sky blue eyes were beaming—at him.

Peter blushed, recalling the great time they'd had last weekend at the play. He'd gone to see her during the week to tell her what a wonderful time he'd had, and to find out if she'd enjoyed herself. Since then he'd wanted to call her every day, but he hadn't. He had to have time to think—to decide.

"You haven't been avoiding me, have you?" Nancy asked jokingly.

"Nah," Peter said. "I've just been buried in work."

Nancy rolled her eyes. "You and everybody else."

Nancy's lips continued to move, but suddenly Peter couldn't hear her. It was the party noise or the noise inside his head as he stood remembering their kiss. He remembered the sweet smell of the perfume she'd been wearing, and the brief, petal-like touch of her hand on the side of his face. And then the thought that maybe things were going a little too quickly. After all, she'd just broken up with her longtime boyfriend, Ned. And then there was Dawn, who was Nancy's resident advisor.

And now there was this. What he couldn't shake. It wasn't going away, and neither was he. . . .

"Hello? Peter? Anybody home?" Nancy was smiling at him.

"Sorry," Peter said.

"Did you hear anything I just said?"

Peter shrugged apologetically.

"I think you've been staring at your computer too long," Nancy said.

Peter smiled, grateful for the excuse. "I do, too."

"Not good for the eyes—or the soul. So, what do you say?" Nancy asked.

"About what?"

Nancy blushed. "I was saying that I was wondering about our second date, the one you mentioned the other day at the newspaper office?"

Peter's eyes slid away guiltily. On the tip of his tongue was the word "Sure." But what he said was, "I—I'd love to, but I'm kind of swamped right now . . . with research," he added unconvincingly.

"Oh," Nancy replied, obviously surprised. "I, um, guess I understand," she murmured.

"Look," Peter said with forced cheer, "by the end of the week, my schedule should lighten up. Maybe Friday—or Saturday."

Nancy looked away. "Sure. Whatever," she said as if she didn't believe him for a second. She started to turn away but then stopped and peered at him. "Is there something wrong?"

"Not at all," Peter said a little too forcefully.

"I mean, we *did* have a great time last week, didn't we?"

"Of course!" Peter almost cried. "Why?"

Nancy shrugged. Her eyes were filled with

questions, but she said, "Just wondering. See you around."

As Nancy weaved back into the crowd, realization hit Peter like a slap across the face: Nancy Drew was the reason he would never love Dawn. Nancy was the girl who was right for him.

And the one girl he couldn't have.

He slipped back into his room and closed the door, grimacing. The disappointment in Nancy's voice still lingered in the air. He wanted to tell her, but it wouldn't be fair to her. Everything was too confused. Everything was happening at once, and too fast.

If only this were another time and place, Peter thought.

But he knew there was too much standing in their way. There was so much Nancy didn't know and couldn't see.

"Maybe if you knew, you wouldn't want to go out with me," Peter thought out loud.

Nancy twisted distractedly through the crowd, stopping every few steps to turn back and eye Peter's closed door. Something's definitely wrong, she said to herself.

Her eyes closed for a second as she pictured his astonishingly handsome face, his intelligent piercing eyes. She still felt the force of his kiss from that night when they accidentally fell into the lake in each other's arms. And then she remembered their wonderfully fun date at the theater.

But it had been a confusing time for her. She and Ned Nickerson had just broken up. Nancy had been with Ned for so long, she'd almost forgotten that other guys existed. Ned had left such a deep hole in her life, that Nancy hadn't had time to consider starting to fill it with someone else. But then Peter came along.

She hardly knew him, and she was never the kind of person to jump into anything, much less a relationship, with her eyes closed. But she couldn't deny the surges of awkward, unexpected emotion. It was pure attraction. Or was it love? Maybe just infatuation? One thing was for sure, she wanted the time to find out.

Is he really busy? Nancy asked herself. Or is he just avoiding me?

"Hey, Nan!"

Nancy smiled weakly as her suitemate Eileen O'Connor put a cup of some unidentifiable liquid in her hand.

"What's this?" Nancy asked unenthusiastically.

Eileen smiled. "Who knows?" She laughed. "Oh, hey, have you seen my roomie anywhere? Reva's never around anymore. It's like living in a single room. I thought I'd like it, but I do miss her."

"All I know is that Reva's been spending most of her time in the computer lab," Nancy replied.

As Eileen was yanked backward into the crowd by some unseen person, Nancy started to inch her way down the hall toward the stairs. She was happy everyone was having a good time, but she'd been looking forward to spending the evening with Peter. And now the evening wasn't as much fun anymore.

"I'll tell you one thing," Nancy heard some guy saying as she got stalled near the stairs. "It's a lot easier when you've already seen the answers."

Whoever the guy was speaking to laughed conspiratorially. "Yeah. I *never* would have passed. But it feels a little weird. You're told all through high school that cheating is the worst crime in the world."

The first guy snorted. "You think you're the only guy in the class who saw that test? Lots of people I know cheat—and just think about all the people I don't know. Frats keep whole file cabinets full of old papers and tests to give out to their brothers. I've seen ads where you can pay someone to write your term paper for you. It's almost like you don't get a fair shot *unless* you cheat. If you can't beat 'em, join 'em."

The second guy cleared his throat, and Nancy quickly pushed on. Up the stairs, leaving the party behind her, she remembered Jake's article. He'd quoted an anonymous Jefferson administrator saying that cheating wasn't a minor problem—it had reached epidemic proportions. In fact, it was probably twice as bad as everyone thought.

If it's bad at Jefferson, Nancy thought outside the door to her suite, it's probably just as bad at Wilder.

*   *   *

"Five, six, seven, eight!" Bess heard the musical director call out from the darkened auditorium at the Hewlitt Theater Arts Complex. For the tenth time that night, her line of dancers shimmied across the stage, snapping their fingers and belting out a single lyric. The rest of the cast was hanging out in the wings in ragged sweats and leotards, tapping their feet to the music.

"Cut!" The director appeared at the lip of the stage. "Looks good, people! Bess, you're really on tonight. What did you do, take happy pills?"

Casey Fontaine and Brian Daglian came in from the wings. "You are really projecting," Casey said admiringly.

Bess wiped at the sweat on her forehead with the back of her hand. "Really, Case?" she asked, still panting from her workout.

"And your smile is *popping,*" Brian added.

Casey appraised her with the seriousness of an expert. "You definitely stand out," she said before heading for the watercooler.

"Coming from a total pro like Casey, that's some compliment," Brian said

"She's just being generous," Bess replied.

"And you're just being modest."

Bess smiled at Brian adoringly. With his sandy blond hair, green eyes, and cute dimples, Brian had a killer combination of all-American good looks and sardonic wit. At first, Bess had been attracted to him, and she thought the feeling was returned—until he confided in her that he was gay. Since then, their bond had gotten even stronger.

With Nancy busy at the newspaper, and George totally wrapped up with Will, Bess relied on Brian more and more.

"So what *is* lighting your fire?" Brian asked.

"I think I did really well on my biology exam today," Bess whispered conspiratorially, then squealed with pleasure. "I mean, I'll never get an A no matter how hard I study, but I think I did good—for me."

"Well, I for one am not surprised," Brian said. "You're as smart as anyone else. You just need a maid. . . ."

The director clapped his hands. In the few seconds of silence as the cast trudged back on stage, Bess heard a smattering of applause and familiar laughter from the back of the auditorium. Raising her arm to her eyes to block out the glare of the lights, Bess squinted into the darkness and gulped. Holly Thornton and Soozie Beckerman were seated in the back row.

Bess was mortified. Holly tried to protect the freshmen pledges from the pranks that Soozie seemed to live to dream up.

They're just here to check out Casey, Bess explained to herself as she took her position in the front line of the chorus.

As the music started up again, Bess started flubbing one dance step after another. Some of the other chorus members acted annoyed with her. Suddenly she noticed the entire cast staring at her and realized that she'd missed a cue. She knew she had a line, but what was it?

"From the top," the director called as everyone else groaned.

Bess pictured Soozie rolling her eyes, and saying stuff like, "I *knew* we shouldn't have let her in Kappa. What a loser!"

Just knowing the two Kappas were there was throwing Bess off. She looked around for Brian. When she saw him, he made a silly face at her, trying to get her to laugh. Then Casey stepped over. "Come on, Bess," she whispered encouragingly in her ear. "Don't think. Just sing. We're all in this together."

Okay, kiddo, Bess prompted herself. Listen to Casey. She's done this a thousand times.

When the music started this time, Bess got into it. She could feel her voice lift easily out of her. Her work was flawless.

"Good job, people," the director called. "But remember, only a few more weeks till opening night!"

They all started collecting their stuff to head out. Soozie and Holly appeared at the lip of the stage.

"Hi," Bess said tentatively.

Holly smiled up at her. "Hi."

Bess grimaced as Soozie grinned devilishly because that grin usually meant trouble.

"Um, Casey's over there—" Bess pointed in the actress's direction.

Soozie didn't reply, but only lifted her hand. Bess's eyes widened with fear. "No," she whispered. "Not here—"

"Yes!" Soozie hissed.

Bess glanced at Holly for support. But Holly only shrugged.

Soozie snapped her fingers twice. Bess winced. The dreaded sign! Whenever a Kappa upperclassman snapped her fingers twice, a pledge had to sing the sorority song at the top of her voice—no matter when, no matter where. Earlier Bess had watched another pledge sing in front of an entire chem lecture! Everyone was howling, including the professor. But not Bess. It was too painful. She was too busy praying it wouldn't ever be her.

Now it was. Alone on the stage. Under the glaring lights. She started to sing alone, weakly: "'Oh, Kappa, sisterhood across the land ...'"

"Louder!" Soozie yelled.

The rest of the cast turned in Bess's direction. "Come on, plebe!" Soozie prodded her. "Sing!"

Out of the corner of her eye, Bess saw Brian, covering his eyes, feeling her humiliation. Casey was barely stifling her laughter. Bess shut her eyes tight and belted out the stupid song at the top of her lungs. It took only a few seconds, but it felt like hours. When she was done, everyone in the auditorium cheered wildly.

By the time Bess opened her eyes, almost everyone had gone—except Brian, who was blushing as deeply as Bess was, and Casey, who was laughing so hard she had to lean against a wall for support.

Bess sat heavily on the stage. "I think I'll go crawl under a rock now," she mumbled.

Inside Suite 301, no one was around.

Everyone's out, Nancy thought. I wonder how Bess did today—

Outside her door, she heard the phone in her room ringing. "Peter," she prayed as she rushed in.

She reached the phone panting. "Hello?"

"Hi, stranger."

It wasn't Peter.

"Ned," Nancy said as the name rolled off her tongue like an old memory. She hadn't really talked to him since their phone conversation two days after they had decided to break off their relationship. That sad realization had happened a few nights after Ned's disastrous visit to Wilder, when they had fought constantly. They both saw that they were heading in different directions.

"Wow," she said, bracing herself. "It feels like it's been a long time."

"Sure does," Ned replied. Nancy thought he sounded good—happy.

"How have you been?" she asked tentatively.

"School's the same. Hard. Lots of work."

"Sounds familiar," Nancy said, commiserating.

"College as hard as you thought?" Ned asked.

"Harder," Nancy responded. She knew her voice was tense. She couldn't identify what she was feeling. It was some version of weird—as if she should be feeling one thing when she was feeling another. They should be saying lovey-dovey things to each other, but they were just chatting, like old friends.

Automatically her hand reached for her throat, where the locket Ned had given her as a going-away present used to hang.

"You okay?" Ned asked with genuine concern. "Did I catch you at a bad time or something?"

Nancy had been standing over her desk the whole time, gripping the phone as if she were afraid it would drop. She let her bag fall to the floor and lowered herself onto her bed, leaning back against her pillows.

"No, I'm fine," she said. "It's just—well, it seems a little strange, talking to you like this." When Ned didn't say anything, Nancy thought she'd insulted him. "Isn't it? Or am I just being stupid?"

Nancy heard Ned laugh softly in an under-standing way. "No," he said thoughtfully. "It *is* strange. But it won't be so strange a week from now, or a month from now—"

"I agree," Nancy said quickly.

"I'm just calling to say hi."

Nancy felt herself smile. "That's nice." She could hear Ned shifting and imagined him getting comfortable on his bed, settling in for a long talk.

"So," he said, "how's life?"

A half hour later Nancy rested the phone back in its cradle. She sat on the end of her bed, her eyes flooded with bittersweet tears. Ned had been totally straightforward about his new life without her. No, the other girls he'd dated weren't as smart as Nancy. Or as pretty. They were well, just different. His whole life was different. Nancy had told him it was the same for her. But they both agreed that *different* meant *good*. It also meant that it was definitely over.

Instinctively, Nancy pictured Peter, just to test herself. She was relieved to feel the same excitement and anticipation.

"But Peter hardly knows me," Nancy thought aloud. And Ned knew what I was going to say before it was out of my mouth. It's so strange to think that it's Ned who knows me better than anyone in the world. Not Peter. Not George or Bess. But Ned, and we aren't in love anymore. We're friends. That's it, she thought wistfully— just friends.

"This is so great!" George cried into Will's ear, clinging to his waist on the back of his motorcycle. They were on a country road far from Wilder. Gently rolling farms and stands of trees whipped by on either side. The moon seemed to be racing them, ducking in and out of the clouds.

George had almost forgotten what the country off campus looked like. This was the first time she'd been away from Wilder since she arrived at the beginning of the semester. Before she met Will. It felt like years ago. She could hardly remember her old life, high school, the faces of old teachers. Even her parents seemed far away.

Tonight, alone with Will, she felt as free as a bird. As if anything could happen.

"Hold on!" Will called back as he banked around a sharp turn. Only trees whizzed by now, a patch of forest on either side lay deep and dark.

Her arms were wrapped tightly around his waist, her cheek pressed against his back as the wind whistled through the ear-holes of her helmet. George could feel Will's warmth against her stomach, the pulse of the motorcycle's engine underneath her. The moon was hanging above them like a peep hole to another universe, another world.

Will slowed and pulled onto the gravel shoulder, letting the bike roll to a stop at a small truck selling burgers and ice cream. A few picnic tables sat hunched in the dark at the edge of the woods.

The only sound was the crickets, chirping like a thousand hearts beating. "Where are we?" George asked, taking off her helmet and fluffing up her hair.

Will took her in his arms. "Nowhere."

They kissed deeply. "That's just where I want to be," George said between kisses.

"Okay, okay," an old cranky voice behind them complained. "I got a weak ticker. You're gonna send me to the hospital. Do you want to eat, or are you still in that phase where you don't need food?"

"I'm starving!" George said excitedly.

"Two burgers," Will said, pulling out his wallet.

George slapped down her money first. "It's on me," she said, winking at the old man. "You drove."

"But I said I'd buy to celebrate acing your exam."

George shrugged playfully. "Just too slow, I guess."

The old man clucked his tongue. "These modern girls. Won't let ya treat 'em right."

"What's this world coming to?" Will said, winking at George.

George jabbed Will playfully. "The problem with *men,*" she said with mock condescension, "is that they don't know a good thing when they see it."

"Oh, *I* know it," Will said, tickling George under the arms. She chased him across the lot toward the picnic tables, where they waited for their food.

"I feel like a kid tonight," George said happily, lying back on the table. Above her, the sky was alive, crawling with galaxy after galaxy. "Look at all those stars! The universe is so huge . . . so amazing."

George could feel Will's gaze on her face. It felt like the sun. "Not as amazing as you," he said.

She looked up at him, and he leaned over her and kissed her again.

Tingling all over, George melted into his arms. "Are you happy?" Will whispered.

George had to keep herself from shrieking with

pleasure. " 'Happy' is not the word. There. Did you see it? The shooting star! Quick, make a wish."

Will clenched his eyes shut longer than George thought he would. She could see him concentrating, the beginnings of a smile lifting the corners of his mouth. Finally he opened his eyes, and George thought she'd just die: huge and black, his eyes were bottomless pools. She wanted to swim in them.

Will took George's hands in his and gripped them hard. His fingers were warm, slick with nervous sweat.

"You know what I wished for?" he asked solemnly.

George didn't need him to tell her. She met his gaze and looked right through his eyes to his heart. She felt waves of different emotions fighting for her attention: fear, then safety—finally, pure love.

It was all happening so quickly, more quickly than she'd ever imagined. During all her daydreams while she was growing up, all her gossipy conversations with Nancy and Bess, had she ever pictured Will to be the one? Did she ever think his name would be Will Blackfeather?

She was growing up. She was responsible. She would be lying if she said she hadn't thought about it. She loved him.

I love him, George thought to herself. *I'm ready.*

"Yes." She gave his hands a squeeze back. "Yes."

CHAPTER 5

"Morning, early bird," Kara squealed as Nancy sat up against her pillows. Kara was standing wrapped in a bath sheet at the dresser mirror. She was throwing out old makeup and hair accessories, and spreading new ones before her like a surgeon's instruments. All the new bottles were brown, and claimed to be environment friendly.

"New stuff?" Nancy asked from bed.

"Did you know that the dyes in most shampoos kill fish in the lakes?" Kara asked, horrified.

"Really?" Nancy replied, as if she hadn't heard it all before. She was amazed at the turnaround Kara had made since getting involved with Wilder's environmental sorority. She'd started getting up at dawn and policing the halls of Thayer, gathering every scrap of paper or plastic—even candy wrappers—in paper bags for recycling. Of course it was a great idea, and Nancy was totally

66

for it. She wanted to be encouraging—but Kara's fervor was starting to get annoying.

"You know what we say in Pi Phi," Kara recited cheerfully. " 'Think Globally, Act Locally.' "

"I'll keep it in mind," Nancy said, and climbed out of bed.

Nancy pulled on her jeans and a shirt and scowled in the mirror.

"Bad hair day," Kara informed her.

"I'll wear a hat to breakfast." Nancy pulled on a maroon Wilder baseball cap and tugged it low over her eyes. "That's better. Ear-to-ear coverage."

Kara dragged out from under the bed a box from Selena's, an expensive boutique downtown, and lifted up a black Lycra micro-mini. She held it up in the mirror, tossing her head and striking a dramatic pose.

"What do you think?"

Nancy raised an eyebrow.

"My present to myself after my first big exam," Kara explained. "It's for my big date."

"Really. With who?" Nancy inquired.

Kara shrugged. "With whoever asks me."

Nancy looked at her and nodded. "Okay," she said, as if that made perfect sense. With Kara, it sort of did. Though she had to admit, the dress would really accentuate Kara's lines.

"But is Lycra environmentally sound?" Nancy wondered out loud.

Kara blushed and squirmed. "Why, s-sure it

67

is," she said, as if she didn't really believe it herself.

"Just asking," Nancy wisecracked.

There was a knock on the door. "Nancy?"

"George?" Nancy opened the door a crack, and George stepped in.

"Want to get some break—" Nancy started to say.

But George had taken her by the hand. "We have to talk."

Nancy stared longingly at the door. "How about over some banana pancakes—"

But George yanked her down on the bed. "It can't wait another second."

George wore an expression Nancy had never seen before. She looked almost possessed. "Should I be concerned?"

"Yes. I mean no!"

"Is it Will?" Nancy asked, suddenly worried.

George nodded, blushing.

"Are you okay?"

George leaned forward. "I need to talk to you"—she nodded in Kara's direction—"alone."

Kara was flitting around the room, tidying up what was obviously already clean, lining up her makeup bottles, refolding her clothes. Definitely not minding her own business, Nancy observed.

Nancy cleared her throat.

"Oh, am I intruding?" Kara asked, feigning surprise. Disappointed, she moved toward the door. "I guess I'm hungry, anyway."

The second the door closed, George shot up

and paced the room. Nancy laughed out loud. She'd never seen her good friend so animated.

"Will took me for a drive on his motorcycle last night," George started to explain.

Nancy smiled. "Cool. Was it romantic?"

"It was straight out of a fairy tale!"

"So you're happy," Nancy concluded.

"We're *more* than happy—"

"In love. *Excuse* me," Nancy corrected herself. "You know about our camping trip, right?"

Nancy nodded. "I've got to hand it to you guys," she said. "You definitely seem suited for each other."

George sat beside Nancy. "That's just what we were thinking," she said seriously.

Nancy could tell George was leading up to something. She asked, only half-kidding, "Will didn't propose to you last night, did he?"

"What makes you say that?" George asked innocently.

"Come on, George!" Nancy rolled her eyes. "Are you going to make me play Twenty Questions?"

George took a big breath and stared her old friend in the eyes. "Will and I decided . . ." she began. Then she stopped and composed herself. "Well, on this camping trip . . . we'd be alone, under the stars. We'd have those sleeping bags . . ."

"And . . ." Nancy prodded.

"And, well, they zip together to make one *big*

bag. . . . And we could be together . . . *very* together."

Nancy froze. She knew this day would come, but she didn't know when, or how, or which of them—her or George or Bess—it would be to take this step first.

In the long seconds that passed before she spoke, Nancy realized that in the back of her mind she'd always assumed it would have been she and Ned. After all, they'd known each other for years, and they'd been in love. Nancy had never felt ready, and Ned never pushed her. A small part of her wondered what would have happened if they *had* slept together.

But now we'll never know, Nancy accepted wistfully.

She could feel a smile creep across her face. "I'm really happy for you, George."

"You are?"

"Of course I am!" Nancy responded. "But are you sure?" Nancy asked. "I want you to be sure."

George nodded firmly. "We talked over everything last night. That's the thing about Will, he's totally up front. That's why I know I can trust him."

"And you love him?"

George nodded.

"Because the first time," Nancy started to say. "I always thought, and we always talked about it, you and Bess and me, about being with somebody you really love. He definitely loves you. I can see that with my own eyes."

"He's the best thing that ever happened to me."

"And he *is* a total hunk," Nancy said, as she and George erupted in nervous laughter.

Nancy could tell George was waiting for her to say something, something she hadn't said yet.

"What do you think, Nan?" George asked.

So that was it, Nancy thought. George wants to know my feelings.

Nancy cleared her throat, remembering the one or two times she and Ned had talked seriously about sleeping together. He'd said that no one else could make that decision for her. Even if he was ready, *she* had to be ready, too. And only *she* would know when she was.

"Have you told Bess yet?" Nancy asked.

George squirmed a second. "Actually, I thought of you first, because you and Ned..." She paused. "Because you had a serious boyfriend, and I figured you and Ned talked about it."

Nancy nodded. She knew what George was saying.

"I just thought you'd have better advice than Bess," George added. "But I am going to tell her."

"Well, to be honest, it doesn't matter what I think," Nancy explained. "I think Will's a great guy. But you have to listen to your own heart and mind. Have fun, but be sure. And safe. You *have* to be safe," Nancy added as she and George hugged each other.

"You're the best friend I could ask for," George said affectionately. "You're right. We're going to talk about it some more, but I love him, Nan. I really do."

"You'll know what to do, George," Nancy told her friend. "You'll know."

"And then Professor Ross's face turned so purple I thought the veins in his neck would burst!" Leslie overheard some girl on her floor say into her phone. "He was sputtering about how everybody cheats, how he can't trust anybody anymore, even the people who work for him."

Leslie shut her door and swallowed hard, her palms sweating. "This can't be happening," she said out loud. "Ginny and I will be the obvious suspects. We're in his office all the time, even when he's not around."

Leslie wanted Ross's attention, but not *this* kind.

I've got to stop him from thinking of me. Even when he finds out I didn't do it, he'll always think of cheaters when he thinks of me.

Leslie paced back and forth across the floor, twirling her blond hair around a finger. She didn't have a single idea.

Every time she passed Bess's side of the room, her arm snapped to her face in a reflex to hide her eyes.

"Slob," Leslie muttered under her breath.

Then she stopped. Something on Bess's bed caught her eye. A piece of paper with some notes jotted down, notes from Ross's bio class. But it wasn't Bess's handwriting. Crossed out on the top half were other notes, from another class. It looked like computer science. And along the very top, crossed out, Leslie could just make out the name: Ginny Yuen.

"Ginny?" Leslie wondered out loud. "Yes. Ginny."

Leslie reached for the phone.

Nancy was walking up the steps of the *Wilder Times* office with two jumbo coffees—one for her, and one for Jake, if he was there, and she was sure he would be. I hope he likes organic coffee, Nancy thought, eyeing the cups warily. Kara had just been badgering her with information she'd gotten at a Pi Phi meeting. They'd said organic coffee not only tasted better, but it was better for the environment—no pesticides, no exploitation of the land. Nancy was dubious, but it did seem to taste better. *And* it had a lot of zip.

Usually just entering the paper's office raised her spirits. But she was still in a quiet funk. She couldn't shake off her earlier conversation with George. For some reason it had put her in a mood. Not a bad one, but a pensive one. George had made her think about herself and when she would be ready to take that huge step. It wasn't only a matter of meeting the right guy, she knew, because she had definitely been in love with Ned.

73

It was something more, a combination of the right guy and something she couldn't put her finger on. Something *inside* her.

"Trust yourself," Nancy advised herself. "Like you told George. You'll know."

"Know what?" a voice asked behind her.

"Oh, hi, Gail," Nancy said. I *really* have to stop talking to myself in here, she thought.

"That profile on Casey Fontaine looks pretty good," Gail said.

Nancy smiled. Could this really be? A compliment from the dour, critical Gail Gardeski? "Thanks," Nancy said, suddenly more glad than ever that she'd bothered to come in early yesterday morning.

"To be honest," Gail said hesitantly, "—and I wouldn't normally say this—it was one of the cleanest articles I've ever received. Which reminds me. Jake mentioned something about giving you a bigger assignment. And I think he might be right about that."

"Really?" Nancy replied excitedly.

"We'll see what stories come along. Keep me informed if you have any ideas."

Nancy swallowed a scream. "I will," she said calmly.

"In the meantime," Gail said, smiling weakly and jamming a sheet of paper under Nancy's arm, "I need some filler blurbs. We're short of feature stories. I need these first thing Monday."

"Gee, thanks, Gail," Nancy said well after Gail had left the office.

Walking toward her cubicle, she noticed a pair of cowboy boots resting on her desk in the shape of a *V.* Jake was sprawled in her chair, sleeping soundly.

Nancy tiptoed over. It's funny, she thought, until yesterday I was so intimidated by Jake. He was so out of my reach. Now he's just a really nice guy—and cute, too, with his serious eyes. I even like the way he leaves his mouth open a bit when he's sleeping.

Nancy grinned as a wild idea passed through her mind: kissing Jake on the lips, like Sleeping Beauty, to wake him up.

Laughing at herself, Nancy took the lid off one of the coffees instead and waved the steaming cup under his nose.

"Hmmm," Jake said groggily. "Fuel." He opened one eye. "Nancy! Just the person I was—"

"Thank you—" Nancy cut him off.

"What did I do now?" Jake asked.

"You talked to Gail."

Jake waved his hand. "Don't mention it. You deserve it. But listen to this." He slid his feet off Nancy's desk and sat up. "The results from Monday's biology exam are in, and the buzz is that the grades were too good to be true."

"Too good—you mean people cheated?" Nancy asked, thinking of the two guys she had overheard the night before.

"Do you know Ross, the bio professor?"

Nancy nodded. "I have a friend in his class."

"Well he's positive his test was swiped. He's calling for an investigation. He won't post any of the results until they figure out what happened. In fact he's threatening to flunk the whole class."

I have to talk to Bess, Nancy thought urgently.

"I *knew* this cheating thing was worse than anyone thought," Jake said with relish. "It *is* an epidemic. It's everywhere!"

Nancy lowered herself onto her desk. "You know, I overheard two guys in my dorm talking about cheating last night. They said everybody does it. In fact, they said that if they *didn't* do it, they couldn't keep up."

"That's great stuff, Nancy!" Jake said, reaching for his notebook. "Who were they?"

Nancy shrugged dejectedly. "I didn't see them."

Jake was disappointed.

"Next time," Nancy promised.

"I'm glad you said that," Jake said, getting to his feet. "Because I want to write a second article on cheating. This time about Wilder, and I want you to help me."

"Me?"

Jake pointed his pencil at her. "You. You're good. We'll be a team."

Nancy felt a charge of electricity surge up her spine. Jake wanted her to work with him. Maybe she could even write a side piece to go with his article. Maybe this was her big break.

"But I have these blurbs," Nancy lamented, holding up the piece of paper Gail had given her.

Jake shrugged, as if saying she had to make a choice. He took a sip of his coffee.

"Good coffee, huh?" Nancy asked.

Jake nodded. "Not bad. What kind is it?"

Nancy considered if Jake was ecology minded or not. She decided he wasn't. Maybe it was the cowboy boots. She shrugged. "I didn't notice. Special of the day."

CHAPTER 6

It figures that the exam I almost melted my brain studying for would be canceled, Bess lamented as she slowly took the stairs up to her floor, hauling herself up by the railing. And I was positive I did really well on this one.

Not only that, she went on, but if Professor Ross flunks everybody, then I could get bounced out of Wilder!

"If I ever get my hand on the cheaters, I'll wring their necks," she muttered as she reached her floor.

She strolled down the hall, pausing outside her open door. It was slightly open, and she could hear Leslie talking to someone inside.

"Hello, Professor Ross? Hi, this is Leslie King," Bess overheard Leslie say in a sickeningly syrupy voice. It was like a little girl's voice, and Bess winced, embarrassed for her—though she had to admit, it was kind of interesting to hear what Leslie was like with people she wanted to impress rather than step on.

"I heard about the cheating," Leslie went on, "and I just wanted to tell you how sorry I am.... Yes, I know you tried your best to prevent it. But, Professor Ross, there's something you should know. Well, I don't know *for sure* that it's information about the cheaters, but I thought it was kind of interesting. Why don't I let you come to your own conclusions...."

What could Leslie possibly know? Bess thought, setting her bag down and moving closer to the door.

"There's someone in that class named Ray Johansson," Leslie went on suggestively. "Right, that punk rocker with the tattoo. He's one of the ones whose grade was incredibly good. Exactly, almost too good to be true. That's my point. There's something about Ray that you should know. His girlfriend is Ginny Yuen."

Ginny? Bess wondered, leaning closer, intensely interested. What was Leslie implying about Ginny?

"Remember when you were telling us about hiding your test on your computer in your office yesterday?" Leslie said. "I happen to know for a fact that Ginny is a computer expert. And one more thing. I hear Ginny has been giving lots of help to a lot of people. That's right, Professor Ross. *Lots* of help. Including to Ray Johansson . . . What kind of help? Well, as you said, I'll let you come to your own conclusions."

Bess swallowed hard. Leslie was accusing Ginny of cheating? But Ginny's been helping me, too! Bess thought. She would never cheat. She's just a great teacher.

"I think that's a good idea," Leslie went on cheerily as though she were making plans for a party. "You should talk to her immediately—if you know what I mean."

Leslie put down the phone. "Poor Ginny," she said.

"Poor Ginny is right," Bess said forthrightly, pushing open the door. For a second Leslie's eyes widened with panic, but as she folded her arms across her chest, they quickly narrowed with anger.

"I didn't know eavesdropping was your style, Bess," Leslie said icily.

At first Bess was paralyzed with rage, fear, and nervousness. She'd never said a harsh word to Leslie in all the time they'd lived together. She'd let Leslie steamroll over her in every argument, make every dig, throw every kind of annoyed glance at her, take every last laugh. Bess had not once stood up for herself. Leslie had been heartless in her criticism of her from the beginning.

Not anymore, Bess decided. This was too much. Ginny wasn't only a friend; she was incredibly generous. She didn't deserve to be stabbed in the back.

"I heard what you told Professor Ross about Ginny," Bess asserted. "That wasn't fair."

Leslie arched an eyebrow. Bess could see she was taken aback by Bess's challenge. Still, all she did was make herself busy tidying her desk.

"That wasn't fair!" Bess raised her voice.

Leslie lifted her head, a smug, plastic smile painted on her face. "It's none of your business," she said, lifting her nose in the air.

"Ginny's my friend," Bess said. "And she should be yours. You work with her."

Leslie shrugged and looked away.

"She's too honest to cheat," Bess insisted. "And you know it."

"Do I?" Leslie replied blithely.

Bess was surprised at how enraged she felt. Three weeks of feeling cowed by Leslie's withering glances had taken its toll.

"Yes, you do," Bess accused. "You don't have any proof that Ginny cheated. You don't even know if Ray did. Maybe he just studied hard. Maybe he really did learn all that material. It's possible, you know." Bess paused, choked up, thinking of how hard she had studied, and how well she was sure she'd done—and all for nothing.

Bess leveled a steady gaze at Leslie. "I don't know why you're doing this to her, Leslie—b-but, but you're selfish, you're mean, and all you care about are your precious plans for medical school!"

Leslie's jaw dropped; tongue-tied, she started to sputter. Bess was sure she'd hit a bull's-eye.

"And I'm not going to let you get away with it!" Bess turned and flew out of the room.

Nancy stared vacantly at the heaps of delicious-looking salads on her plate. Glistening three-bean, nutritious arugula, creamy gobs of potato. Steering the beans around with her fork, she absently made designs across her plate. She couldn't eat.

The Thayer Hall cafeteria was packed. At the salad bar, Nancy had overheard a few people from the biology class gossiping about the cheating scandal. There were rumors ranging from the Jefferson College computer hackers hatching a plot at Wilder to Wilder's own president leaking Professor Ross's exam because he didn't like him.

"And you're a talented artist, too," a familiar voice said over her shoulder.

Nancy quickly wiped out the designs with her fork as Jake plopped his tray down next to hers. "Hello," Nancy said, embarrassed.

Jake shook his head at Nancy's wasted food. "I guess you know about all the starving children in India."

"My roommate's been telling me about it night and day," Nancy threw back.

After a beat or two of silence, Nancy said, "Well, your article sure made a hit. Everyone's talking about it."

"Good timing." Jake shrugged, picking up his

knife and fork. "Did you finish those blurbs?" he asked between bites.

Nancy sighed. "Gail left a mountain more on my desk just before I left."

"That's too bad," Jake said, and this time Nancy was sure he meant it. "I looked forward to working with you. Next time, maybe."

"I did think your writing could use a little spice," Nancy said with a jesting wink.

Jake paused midchew. "Is that a challenge? Because I love a challenge."

"He sure does," said a voice above them.

They both looked up. "Pete!" Jake cried.

Nancy looked back and forth between them, amazed. "You know each other?"

"Since freshman year," Peter said, putting down his tray. "We were roommates."

"I know it's hard to believe," Jake said confidingly in Nancy's ear, but loud enough for Peter to hear. "We couldn't stand each other. He was a slob. All he ate was pizza."

Nancy laughed uneasily. No one needed to say that Jake was talking about himself.

"Nancy, meet—" Jake started to introduce them.

"We already have."

Jake glanced at Nancy over his fork. "Oh?"

"I live on the floor below," Peter explained.

Nancy smiled at Peter, but he just flashed her a weak grin.

Something's definitely wrong, Nancy thought, trying to make meaningful eye contact with

Peter. What did I do? One day he kisses me and tells me I'm great, and now he looks right through me.

"See what you did?" Peter said to Jake, gesturing to the lunch crowd. "Always making trouble."

Nancy laughed, a little too loudly, trying to catch Peter's attention. But he didn't really respond. *He's pretending nothing ever happened between us,* she thought dismally.

It was starting to upset her, but she couldn't deal with it right then. She had too much on her mind. For one thing, she had to talk to Bess to see how she was dealing with the cheating in bio.

"I have to go," she announced, standing, all the time hoping Peter would ask her to stay. Peter didn't—he was too busy stirring his baked ziti into soup—but Jake did. "Sorry," Nancy apologized, not taking her eyes off Peter.

"Good luck with the article," she said to Jake, and turned to leave. Just as she did, Peter finally raised his head to look at her. But what she saw confused her even more: the expression in Peter's eyes was a mix of desire and fear.

"When do you think they'll post the results?" Ray asked excitedly, pacing across Ginny's floor.

Standing on her toes, Ginny wrapped her arms around his neck. "Patience. Professor Ross said he puts them up exactly twenty-four hours after the exam. I'm so happy for you!" she squealed.

Ginny was elated. She'd never seen Ray so

happy about anything having to do with school. It just proved her point that all Ray's talk about not caring about grades was just a cover. He just didn't know how to be a good student.

But he does now! Ginny thought. "Here's to hard work," she said, toasting Ray with a container of orange juice.

"Wait!" Ray dashed across his room and got a can of soda out of the small refrigerator Ginny kept in the corner. He shook it and popped the tab, and he and Ginny giggled as the soda foamed out like champagne. "Here's to me," he said, raising it up.

Ginny closed in. "Here's to you," she said, her voice sultry, her eyes focused on his lips. . . .

As they embraced, they dropped their drinks on the floor. It was the most passionate kiss Ginny had ever had. As Ray's strong hands pressed against her back, she lost herself in time and place. The words "I love you," words they'd never exchanged, rose to her lips. She was just about to say them when the phone rang.

"Go away," she whispered, and kissed Ray harder.

"Go ahead and get it," Ray said. "I'm not going anywhere."

"Don't move a muscle," Ginny said, withdrawing from Ray's arms. She picked up the phone. "Hello?"

"Are you Ginny Yuen?" an older woman wanted to know.

"Can I help you?" Ginny asked.

A sudden chill ran up Ginny's spine. The woman on the other end was all business, her voice flat and official. The only time people called like this was to sell something—or deliver bad news.

"Is anything wrong?" Ginny asked tentatively.

"Ginny?" she heard Ray call behind her.

"Then you *are* Ginny Yuen," the woman confirmed.

"Who else would I be?" Ginny replied impatiently. "Is it my parents? Are they okay?"

"This has nothing to do with your parents," the woman said. "The dean of students would like to see you, at once."

Ginny threw a scared glance at Ray, who came to stand by her side.

"May I ask what this is about?" Ginny requested.

"Well, I'm not at liberty to say."

Ginny was panicking. My loan, she thought. Something went bad with my loan! "Do I owe money, or something?"

"Just come down to the dean's office, please," the woman said curtly. "He'll be waiting."

Ginny put down the phone, stunned. A thousand things that could possibly be wrong flashed through her brain, but she couldn't settle on a single one. "The dean of students wants to see me."

"Why?"

"I don't know," Ginny said worriedly. "I don't know."

*   *   *

"Isn't she great?" Jake said to Peter after Nancy was out of earshot.

Peter could only nod as Nancy moved away through crisscrossing lines of hungry freshmen. He knew she was angry, or at least confused. He wanted to tell her the truth. But just when he felt himself opening up to someone, he shut down. He couldn't even tell Jake, his oldest friend at Wilder.

"Hello?" Jake snapped his fingers in front of Peter.

Peter blinked. "Sorry," he said.

Jake leaned forward. "I know you're having a hard time," he said gently.

"You do?" Peter said warily.

"And I think I know what it is."

"You do?" Peter repeated, suddenly afraid he'd let something slip.

"I've always liked Dawn," Jake disclosed as if he thought this was the problem. "I told you that yesterday. So if you want to talk it out with me, maybe I can help you two work things out."

Peter was shaking his head, smiling ironically.

"It's just a thought," Jake offered earnestly. "I'm here if you want me."

"Thanks for the offer," Peter replied. "But I'll pass."

"Okay." Jake held out his hands. "Whenever you're ready."

"Whenever I'm ready," Peter replied evasively. "So," he asked, changing the subject, "how do you know Nancy?"

Jake smiled broadly. "Did I tell you, or what?"

"Tell m-me?" Peter stammered. "You mean Nancy's the woman—"

Jake was nodding. "Yup. She's the one I was talking about yesterday. Isn't she hot?"

"Hot?" Peter echoed, his own blood simmering.

"Do you think I have a chance?"

Peter nudged his tray to the side with a grimace. He was heartsick. He wanted Nancy but couldn't have her. He thought Nancy wanted him, but she couldn't have him. Now his best friend was interested in her. Nancy was the center of a complicated web of love, and she didn't even know it!

"And she's smart," Jake said, bragging. "I can tell nothing gets by her."

Want to bet? was on the tip of Peter's tongue.

"So tell me, what do you think she'd prefer, skydiving or bungee-jumping?"

Peter looked at his friend, partly envious of him and partly helpless.

If you only knew, he mused. If you only knew.

CHAPTER 7

"Bess, where *are* you?" Nancy sighed, pushing open the door to her suite. She hadn't been able to find Bess anywhere. She'd checked out Java Joe's, Bess's favorite hangout. Out of desperation, she'd even made a sweep through the study carrels at the library, even though Bess claimed to suffer from a rare allergy to the dust that collected on library books.

Earlier, at Jamison Hall, Bess's dorm, she'd found only Leslie, who was unusually cold. Typically, when Nancy asked her where Bess might be, Leslie would shrug and make some crack about Bess probably being off at a party or something. They'd chat politely about the weather, just to keep the peace, and then Nancy would leave. Today Leslie had barely acknowledged Nancy's presence. She'd had a weird, shell-shocked expression on her face.

Poor Bess, Nancy thought. Not only does she have a human ice cube for a roommate, but now she's got a serious academic crisis on her hands. I know she needs my support. But where *is* she?

As Nancy strolled through the lounge toward her room, she noticed Stephanie, who barely threw her a nod from the couch.

"Hi, Stephanie," Nancy said with false cheer. "How're classes going?"

"Classes?" Stephanie touched her chin as if she'd never heard of the word.

"That's what I thought," Nancy wisecracked. Turning to leave, she noticed a scrap of paper on the floor next to the couch. "What's that?"

"Oh," Stephanie said blithely, her eyes fluttering closed. "A message from Bess. She called on the lounge phone a little while ago. She said she'd tried your room first. I guess it's urgent."

"Stephanie!" Nancy said, irritated, and picked up the message. It just said "Bess—emergency." "Great message," she mumbled. "Weren't you going to give this to me?"

"If I was awake," Stephanie replied groggily.

"Did she say where she was, when she'd call back?"

Stephanie waved. "I was half asleep."

Crumpling the message and tossing it over her shoulder, Nancy stalked off. "One of these days," she called behind her, "you're going to need our help—and we're *all* going to be taking naps!"

Putting her key in her lock, Nancy heard the suite door bang open and unsteady footsteps approach. A stifled sob filled the air. "Bess?" she wondered out loud.

But it was Ginny who turned the corner, her face streaked with tears, her eyes red and swollen.

"Ginny! What happened?"

Ray opened the door to Ginny's room and stood waiting for her. "Gin!" he cried, and Ginny ran to him and into his arms.

"What's going on?" Nancy cried, totally confused. Everyone she knew—Bess, Peter, and now Ginny and Ray—seemed to be steeped in disaster.

"What did the dean want?" Ray asked gently.

"The *dean?*" Nancy asked.

"He called me in for a meeting," Ginny explained tearfully. She looked up at Ray. "Oh, Ray," she sobbed. "I have really bad news. That test you took, the one you did really well on? They're going to cancel it!"

"B-but—why?" Ray asked, clearly upset.

"Because someone cheated. I mean, a *lot* of people cheated. Or at least that's what they think. Some people who've been doing badly so far this semester got good grades. The only way Professor Ross could explain it was that they saw the test before Monday."

"So I'll just take it again," Ray said with a shrug. "It's just a test."

"But they might fail everybody!" Ginny wailed.

"That's not fair," Nancy murmured. "You

91

can't punish everyone for what a few idiots did."
She thought of the two guys she'd overheard at
the party Monday night. Now I *really* wish I saw
who those guys were! she seethed silently.

"But why did the dean call you in just to tell
you that?" she asked.

"Yeah, what does it have to do with you?"
Ray added.

Ginny's face bunched up. A fresh batch of
tears flooded down her cheeks. "Oh, Ray. They
say they're sure *you're* one of the ones who
cheated!"

"Me?" Ray stepped back, smiling in disbelief.

"Somehow they found out that we were going
out, and they think that I helped you."

"But you did help me, Ginny," Ray said
gently.

"They think I gave you the answers to the
test!"

Nancy gasped, horrified. "You?"

"That's the stupidest thing I ever heard." Ray
laughed. "You cheat? You wouldn't even know
how."

"That's what I told the dean!" Ginny sobbed.
"But he wouldn't believe me. He said that since
I do work-study for Professor Ross, I'm in his
office all the time and would have a lot of oppor-
tunities to see things I shouldn't see. And Ross
talked to me and Leslie King the other day about
how he was going to hide his tests and notes on
the computer."

"Leslie?" Nancy echoed, her curiosity more piqued.

"But Ross didn't tell us exactly *how* he would do it," Ginny complained.

"Did you tell the dean that?" Nancy asked.

Ginny nodded. "He didn't believe me." She shook her head dejectedly, then looked up at Ray with deep love in her eyes. "Ray, they just don't know what kind of guy you are. They don't know you'd never cheat."

"I'd rather fail," Ray said under his breath. The color of his face went tomato red. Nancy could see he was getting angrier by the second.

Ginny sniffed. "They suspended my work-study until they clear this up. So I don't have any money. And if they decide I'm guilty, they're going to expel me."

Nancy held her breath. "Oh, Ginny!"

Ray punched the wall in rage.

Just then the door to the suite opened and Bess appeared in the hallway.

"Nancy, am I glad to see *you!*" Bess cried. "I've been looking all over for you. You're never going to believe what—" She stopped when she saw Ginny and Ray.

"I know," Nancy said, leading Bess over to Ginny and Ray. "Someone cheated on your bio exam, and now everyone might fail."

Bess nodded. "But that's not all," she said.

"I know," Nancy said.

"Wait, you have to listen!" Bess cried.

Everyone turned to Bess. She was breathless.

"Ginny, have you spoken to the dean or Professor Ross yet?"

Ginny cocked her head. "How did you know that?"

"I overheard Leslie making a phone call to Professor Ross," Bess explained. She told them what Leslie had said about Ginny possibly being behind the cheating.

"But why would she do that?" Ginny pondered out loud. "Why would she want to frame *me?*"

"I have my own ideas about that," Bess offered.

Well, that explains Leslie's strange coldness earlier, Nancy realized.

"The funny thing is," Ginny said, shaking her head in amazement, "I know something about computers, but what Ross would use is too advanced for me. I don't know enough—not half as much as Reva does, for instance."

"Reva," Nancy said. Of course! she thought. Our resident computer whiz . . .

Ginny nodded, her tears finally drying up. "Yeah. She's working on that Internet thing. If she doesn't know, she'd know somebody who does."

Nancy's brain was racing a mile a minute, trying to piece everything together. Leslie was falsely accusing Ginny. But why? Nancy wondered whether Leslie could have done the cheating herself. She was nasty and uptight, but she seemed brutally honest. Maybe she was envious of Ginny. Now, *there* was a potential explanation.

"I need a nap," Ginny said, holding her head. She looked as if she might cry again. Ray took her by the shoulders and, massaging them, led her into her room.

Bess turned to Nancy. "What are we going to do?"

"I need to think," Nancy said, feeling fatigued all at once. The person she would have liked to talk this through with was totally avoiding her. Darn you, Peter.

"I know what we need to do," Bess said, suddenly full of energy. "You and I need to have a little chat with Professor Ross first thing tomorrow morning."

"*Me* and you?"

"He knows me, Nancy, but you're better at this stuff than I am. I need you with me."

"But what will we say?"

"I don't know yet." Bess squinted at the wall.

"I don't know, Bess." Nancy shifted her feet. "Do you really think talking to Ross is a good idea? He doesn't seem exactly approachable."

"Oh, he's not," Bess said. "But I *know* I passed that test. And I was looking forward to showing my parents a good grade on that exam. If Ross flunks the whole class, my grade point average is going to disappear. I'll have enough trouble passing the really big exams, and maybe this'll make me flunk the entire semester. But it's not just me—it's other people, too."

Nancy nodded firmly. "Okay. You've convinced me. What time?"

"Ross has office hours at ten o'clock."

The door to Dawn's single creaked open, and Dawn came stumbling of her room, stretching and yawning.

Nancy shook her head. Why was everybody sleeping so much?

Dawn took one look at Nancy's face and instantly woke up. "What happened?"

"Have a seat, Dawn," Nancy said. "I'll explain, but you'll want to be sitting for this one."

Across campus, he was surfing through the computer files he wanted. Professor McCall's class notes for Investigative Journalism 100. Then grade lists for English 414 with Professor Herrin.

"Let's see, would you like me to change your B-plus to an A-minus, Mr. John Atkins?"

Now the Intro to Physics final exam. "I could make a *fortune* selling this one," he said.

He tapped on his keyboard, and spotted a file labeled University President—Coded.

"Coded?" He snickered and made a few keystrokes. "As—easy—as—*pie!* Coded no more!"

The information scrolled up the screen: the secret agenda for the next meeting with the university trustees.

He whistled in amazement. "The possibilities are endless. I could branch out, make this a real business."

He shook his head. "Nope. Cool out, buddy," he scolded himself. "Don't get cocky—or greedy. You'll get yourself caught. Everyone's already talking about the cheating. He laughed ruefully. "It's not like I'm cheating more than anyone else—it's just that I'm more creative. Besides, this isn't cheating. This is justice!"

"Okay, big guy, showtime," Jake taunted, crouching in front of Peter.

They were alone on the sprawling floor of the massive Sage Field House. Surrounding the basketball court where the Wilder team played were six other hoops, a practice area for shot-putters, and a quarter-mile track. Steep rows of bleachers climbed halfway to the ceiling. But now, Wednesday around suppertime, they had the whole, cavernous building to themselves.

They needed it. Jake was dying of curiosity. What was Dawn talking about the other day? And why was Peter so glum lately?

Thinking about it, he'd realized that he had sensed there was something Peter had been keeping from him. About a year ago, something about Peter had changed. He laughed a little less. He kept to himself a little more. He went home a few extra weekends a semester. Jake couldn't put his finger on anything specific, but he knew there was something wrong.

His remedy was a game of one-on-one. During freshman year, they'd played all the time and confided in each other in real heart-to-hearts. They hadn't played in over a year, though. Jake was busy at the paper, and Peter was buried in premed classes. But it had always been the best way to loosen Peter up—not only his mind, but his tongue.

"Okay, big boy," Jake said. "Bring it on!"

Peter's dribbling filled the space with echoes. He circled the ball around his back, through Jake's flailing hands, and bolted for the basket.

"Two points!" Peter cried, raising his arms in victory after dropping in an easy layup.

"Beginner's luck," Jake seethed. He loved the competition. But five minutes later it was Jake who was doubled over, the ball on his hip. "Lookin' sloppy, Goodwin," he cracked.

Suddenly Peter popped the ball out of Jake's grasp and ran it in for an easy basket. "Game, Goodwin!" he cried, grinning from ear to ear. He flipped Jake the ball. "One more?"

"On one condition," Jake said. "Loser reveals his deepest, darkest secret."

A strange glow came to Peter's eyes. "I have a better idea. Winner gets a date with Nancy Drew."

Jake frowned. Why is he interested in her? he wondered. Doesn't he have enough female problems? "Isn't your plate a little full?" he asked.

Peter pounded the ball on the floor. "Jealous?"

"Maybe," Jake replied. "I like the secret idea better. Loser tells all."

Peter sighed. "If I win, you'll get off my back?"

"Why not?" Jake said, sure that this time he'd win.

Ten minutes later the game was tied at ten with a point to go. It was the hardest game they'd ever played. Jake knew that whatever was on Peter's mind was serious, because he had never seen Peter play so furiously. Both of them were struggling for breath. Suddenly Peter snatched the ball, circled Jake, and dumped it in.

"Game," Peter puffed hoarsely, and started walking away across the track, limping, alone.

Totally drained, Jake fell to one knee. "What are you keeping from me?" he called out after him.

Peter only threw up his hands, as if saying, That's for you to figure out.

You're lucky I'm your friend, Jake silently addressed Peter's back. But how good a friend can I be if you won't trust me?

CHAPTER 8

Bess stood underneath a huge maple tree in the middle of the college quad, tightening her jacket against the cool of the early morning. She ran her fingers through her still-wet blond hair, wishing she'd taken more time to dry it. There was a nip in the air, and the grass in the shadows was still white from a light early-morning frost.

She squinted up at the huge and stately classroom buildings across the grassy field, shielding her eyes as the low sun glinted off the dark red-brick fronts and granite columns. The lush green ivy crawling up the sides almost glowed.

"Wilder sure is beautiful," Bess said aloud, a little mournfully. She was still plagued by her fear that the bio exam was going to affect her entire grade-point average. "I just have to get another shot at that exam," she said.

"Where is she?" she murmured to herself,

glancing at the campus clock tower. It was a few minutes before ten. She and Nancy wanted to be first at Ross's office.

Two figures appeared underneath the big arch at one end of the quad: Nancy and a girl with an unmistakable easy stride and shock of red hair. "Oh great, that's all I need—Casey."

Bess was still mortified over her humiliation the other night at the *Grease!* rehearsal. She wanted to join the Kappa sorority more than anything, but she was beginning to wonder whether it was worth the constant embarrassment. And now Casey thinks I'm a total dork, Bess thought, as she watched Nancy and Casey approach. "Smile," she commanded herself. "Now wave." Bess lifted her hand halfheartedly.

"Hey, Casey, you want to come on over to Kappa house today and hang out for a while?" Bess blurted out the second Nancy and Casey were within earshot.

Way to go Bess, she thought through a tight smile. Overanxious, silly . . .

She couldn't believe Casey's simple, one-word reply: "Maybe."

Bess almost jumped out of her skin. "Really?"

Casey shrugged. "Why not? I have some time to kill later. Just keep Soozie Beckerman away from me." She laughed good-naturedly.

Bess grabbed Casey's hand. "That's just great, Case!" she sputtered. "I'm totally psyched!"

"Whatever." Casey gave Nancy a what's-the-big-deal look.

"And I'm sorry about the other night," Bess explained.

Casey didn't get it. "The other night?"

"At the *Grease!* rehearsal. That stupid singing—"

"Bess?" Nancy interrupted. "Don't we have to be someplace?"

"Sure, Nan, whatever you say—"

"Sorry to hear about the bio exam," Casey said understandingly, but she looked a little uncomfortable.

"Thanks, Casey," Bess replied.

Casey smiled tightly.

Nancy cleared her throat. "Bess? Let's go," Nancy said, taking Bess's elbow.

" 'Bye, Casey!" Bess tossed over her shoulder, but Casey didn't hear. She had already walked off.

"Okay, ready or not, here we come," Nancy muttered as she and Bess knocked on Professor Ross's office door in Johnson Hall.

"Come!"

Nancy was surprised by the butterflies in her stomach as they walked into the office. Though she wasn't usually nervous in most situations, she was now.

It's because so much is at stake, she told herself.

Scientific encyclopedias and journals lined the shelves on one wall. A new-looking computer monitor was set up in the far corner.

Ross was just hanging up his coat. "Very punctual," he said. He motioned for Nancy and Bess to take two chairs across his desk. "And you are?"

"Bess Marvin," Bess volunteered. "And Nancy Drew."

"Marvin—yes." Ross nodded. "I recognize the name. But Drew I do not—"

"I'm a friend," Nancy said quickly.

Ross raised his eyebrows. "Of whose?"

"Of mine and Ginny Yuen's," Bess said.

"Ginny Yuen." Ross narrowed his eyes. "You're not here to ask a question about biology, then?"

"Well, actually—I mean—" Bess stalled.

Nancy cleared her throat. "We're here to talk about the exam—and Ginny. You see, we're sure Ginny had nothing to do with the cheating."

"I'm not sure it's any of your business," Ross said haughtily. "It's in the hands of the dean now. Besides, my information came from a very good source."

"I know what that source is," Bess interjected. "I live with her—Leslie King. I know what she told you, and it just isn't true."

Professor Ross brought his fingers together just under his chin. "And you have proof?"

"N-no," Bess stammered. "But I can tell you that Ginny is a talented teacher."

"*Is* she?" Ross replied, leaning forward with sudden interest.

Smiling hard at Ross, Nancy kicked Bess's foot

under the desk to get her to stop talking, but Bess was on a roll.

"Yes," Bess continued. "Ginny was also tutoring me."

Ross was nodding. "So you, too."

"Yes!" Bess said proudly. "And because of her I'm sure I did the best in my life. Otherwise, I would have failed."

"Is that so," Ross muttered suspiciously as he made a note. "Marvin," he said slowly, spelling it out. "I'll have to see just how talented a teacher Miss Yuen is."

Bess was smiling smugly, but Nancy was wincing. Bess didn't see that she'd just dug Ginny's hole deeper—not to mention her own.

"What Bess is *trying* to say," Nancy said quickly to cover Bess's blunder, "is that Ginny is totally honest. She *did* help other students, but only by explaining to them what they didn't understand."

"That's not what I'd call proof on Miss Yuen's behalf," Ross said.

"With all due respect, sir," Nancy said, "what you have isn't proof, either. By your theory, Leslie King could be as much a suspect as Ginny. Though I'm sure neither of them is guilty."

A troubled look crossed Professor Ross's eyes, and Nancy guessed that he wasn't nearly as certain about Ginny as he was acting.

"Do you have any idea how someone might have stolen your exam, Professor Ross?" she probed.

"Let me be frank," he replied. "Cheaters are getting more and more imaginative."

Nancy shook her head in agreement. Ross was very troubled by the rash of cheating. He just wanted it stopped.

"I don't know a great deal about computers," he went on, "but I knew enough to protect myself—or so I thought. No one broke into this office, I'm sure of that. However it was done, it was from outside. And Ginny Yuen was sitting right where you are now when I explained what I had done. She seemed to be quite an expert about encryption codes and such—"

Outside? Nancy wondered. Through an outside computer?

Ross stood abruptly. "I've said too much already. You're just students, after all."

At the door, though, Ross was looking very troubled, and Nancy could tell that he wanted to talk. "One thing is for sure," he said, more to himself than to them, "I won't be using my wife's name as a password again. Too bad, it's beautiful. *Liana*—how could anyone have guessed it?"

Outside the building, Nancy would have laughed at Bess if so much wasn't at stake.

"I really blew it, didn't I?" Bess said sulkily.

Nancy couldn't disagree. "You just gave yourself one more reason to find the cheater. Now Ross suspects you, too."

Seeing that Bess was on the verge of tears, Nancy rested a hand on her shoulder. "Don't worry," she said soothingly. "I know who we need to talk to next."

"You do?" Bess asked hopefully.

"Did you hear what he said about his password?"

Bess shrugged. "So?"

Nancy chuckled. "You don't know much about computers, do you?"

"Not really."

Nancy strode off in the direction of Thayer Hall as Bess stood disconsolately on the steps of Johnson. "Don't worry, Bess," Nancy called back. "I know someone who does!"

Nancy had no problem spotting Reva at Java Joe's. Typically, she wouldn't be able to hear herself think, and the overflow customers would be sprawled out on the wide steps outside. But today, only a couple of tables were taken.

"Thanks for meeting me on such short notice," Nancy said, sliding into the booth opposite Reva with her cappuccino.

"I needed some air, anyway," Reva said. "Down in the computer lab, there's no way to tell whether it's day or night. One day last week, Andy and I totally lost track of time and forgot to sleep. When we finally left, the sun was just coming up."

Nancy nodded. "Eileen says you're hardly around anymore. She says it's like having a single."

Reva sighed as she sagged back against the

booth. "You get caught up in the computer world, and you forget what the real one is like," she mused.

"So how *is* your project coming?" Nancy inquired.

Reva leaned forward excitedly. "Working with Andy is great. He's a total genius at this stuff!"

Nancy winked. "And not bad looking, either, huh?"

"Why, I have no idea what you're talking about," Reva deadpanned. Then she broke out in laughter. "Well, that is an extra benefit—but the guide's going to be really good. I'm really proud of it."

"I have to admit," Nancy said, choosing her words carefully, "I don't really understand computer networks that well myself, especially the Internet."

Reva nodded knowingly. "No one thinks they do. But the whole thing is really simple. It's like learning a foreign language. Once you have the basic lingo down, you're off and running. That's what we're trying to get across in the guide."

Reva sipped her coffee. "So—why am I here?"

"You've heard about Ginny and the cheating scandal."

Reva tilted her head. *"Ginny?* What are you talking about? She'd never do anything like that."

"Well, brace yourself," Nancy said. She told Reva the whole story.

"Wow." Reva whistled after Nancy finished. "I *have* been underground too long."

When she told her what Professor Ross had said about trying to hide his exam on his computer, Reva guffawed. "I don't know that much about computer theft, but I do know that there are tons of ways to break into someone's computer files. Especially if the person protecting his files doesn't know much about computer security. And it sounds like he didn't."

"Really?" Nancy never knew what a whiz Reva was at this stuff.

"Well," Reva continued, "think of breaking into a computer file as breaking into a house. There's the stuff you want to steal, which is the computer file—in this case, the bio exam. There's the lock, which is whatever security system you use. And there's the key—except with computers, there are a lot of keys. You find the right key, and you're in."

Nancy nodded. "I get it. But wait—what do you mean, the key?"

"The key is a password, like Open Sesame," she answered. "Except Open Sesame is sort of out of style."

Nancy leaned forward. "So what are some ways to break in?"

"I know a few of them," Reva said, "but I know someone who knows them all. Andy. He probably knows more about computers than anybody on campus—"

Nancy looked up as Ginny sprinted through the door, out of breath.

"Nancy, I've been looking for you all over campus! I have good news—I think." Ginny slid into the booth beside Reva and put a manila envelope on the table. "Ray found this outside his door just before the exam on Monday, but he didn't open it until now. He thought it was just fan mail."

Nancy's eyes widened. "What is it?"

Grinning, Ginny slid the envelope across the table. "Open it."

"It's Ross's bio exam! But how—who—"

"Exactly." Ginny breathed a sigh of relief. "Ray didn't see it beforehand. We found that together as we were leaving for biology class the day of the test. Whoever stole that exam wasn't me, and that proves it."

Nancy's mind kicked into high gear. "I wonder if anyone else got one of these," Nancy pondered.

"I doubt whoever did would admit it," Reva replied.

Nancy nodded. "You're probably right."

"Did Bess?" Ginny asked.

Nancy shook her head. "She would have told me."

"But this definitely clears Ray and me, don't you think?" Ginny appealed.

"Well, sort of—" Nancy said gingerly.

Ginny's dejection was all over her face. "Why only 'sort of'?"

"Because *I* believe you're telling the truth, Ginny, but I doubt the administration will. I talked to Professor Ross this morning. He seems more interested in finding someone to blame than in catching the real cheater."

Nancy saw Ginny deflate like a pricked balloon. "Don't worry," she assured her. "We'll figure it out."

"But how?" Ginny moaned.

Suddenly Nancy remembered what Reva had said about Andy. At first she was excited. Andy would help them track down the computer thief. Then a new idea came to mind. Reva said he knew more about computers than anyone on campus. He knew all about passwords, for instance. Nancy wondered, could Andy Rodriguez, Will's roommate and Reva's friend, possibly be the one they were looking for?

"I think it's time to talk to Andy about this," Nancy said.

CHAPTER 9

Bess!" the girl whispered from behind her, "Stop looking around, or you'll get us all in trouble!"

Grimacing and flushing scarlet, Bess marched on, sandwiched between two other Kappa pledges, Barbara, whom she really liked, and Susan, whom she didn't think she *should* like—mostly because Soozie Beckerman did.

They were walking in lockstep across the quad, eyes forward, totally mute—just another one of the little chores Soozie dreamed up.

The only problem was, Bess couldn't help looking at all the people who were calling out to them—and laughing at them. It was noon, and classes had let out just at the moment they were filing by. Everyone was applauding as though they were at a parade.

Bess wanted to march right under a rock and keep marching.

Please be over soon, Bess pleaded. Please don't let anybody I know see me. I don't get it—other girls are pledging sororities, but why does it seem that the Kappas are the only ones who make us do this stuff? Will life in Kappa house be worth all these weeks of total stupidity?

Bess had to admit it: she was beginning to regret pledging a sorority. She didn't have time to study or be with her friends. And these ridiculous stunts!

"Hi, Bess," she heard from the steps beside her. Against the rules, she turned her head, then snapped it forward again.

Casey!

Bess was helpless. She wasn't allowed to talk to anyone—another dumb rule.

What am I supposed to do, just walk by?

That's just what she did, blushing with embarrassment and frustration.

In the safety of the other end of the quad, after she'd already been laughed at so many times she'd lost count—Bess took the chance of glancing behind her. She spotted Casey's tall, willowy frame and distinctive short hair on the steps of the library, and watched her longingly.

"That was fun!" Barbara squealed.

Bess swallowed hard. "I guess so, if you're a glutton for punishment."

"Yeah, let's walk back," Susan agreed.

Bess rolled her eyes. "I don't think so."

How am I supposed to get Casey interested in

Kappa if Kappa keeps making us do silly stuff like this?

As Reva led the way through the rooms of the computer lab, Nancy was surprised at how depressing it was. First of all, it was underground, which meant that the only light came from long buzzing bars of fluorescent lights. The walls were blank and the floor a dingy gray. An old vending machine in the hallway sold candy bars. Other than the people bent over the dozens of computer terminals, there were no other signs of life.

"Nice place, huh?" Reva cracked, obviously sensing Nancy's surprise.

"I guess it's not a bad place to concentrate on computer stuff, right?" Nancy offered.

"To be honest, once I'm working on a computer, either on a paper, or going on-line with the Internet, I may as well be in Timbuktu. I have no idea *where* I am."

She led Nancy through room after room, until they reached one small one with bigger and newer computers. When Nancy spotted Andy hunched over a terminal in the far corner, she was astounded. It was true she hadn't seen him in the last couple weeks, but the Andy she remembered was clean-cut and distinctively handsome. This guy was surrounded by empty candy wrappers and soda cans. His eyes were bloodshot, he was wearing an old T-shirt, and he looked as if he hadn't shaved in days.

"Hi, Andy," Nancy said uncertainly as she and Reva pulled up chairs.

Andy practically jumped out of his seat. "You scared me!" he said.

"Where's Stuart?" Reva asked.

Andy waved his hand. "He just took off." Then he spun back to the keyboard and began typing furiously. The screen changed and changed again.

Reva squinted at the monitor. "That's not what we've been working on, is it?"

When the screen went blank, Andy seemed to relax. "No—just some other stuff. Anyway," he said, turning to Nancy, "what brings you down here?"

"Nancy has some questions for you," Reva explained.

Nancy couldn't be sure, but she thought she saw a flicker of something in Andy's eyes. Fear, maybe?

"Just some general stuff," she assured him.

"So what do you want to know that Reva couldn't tell you?" Andy challenged her.

"We were just wondering about passwords and encryption codes and stuff," Reva said. "You said you'd tell me, but we never seem to get around to it."

"But why?" he asked. "We don't have enough time, and there are more important things to concentrate on."

Nancy shrugged. "I just wanted to know how passwords work," she said, "and how somebody might break through a secret code to get to a certain file, that's all."

"That's *all?*" Andy almost laughed. "That would take all day to explain!"

"She doesn't want to do it herself, Andy," Reva said, coming to Nancy's rescue. "She just wants to know the basics."

Andy fidgeted in his chair. He looked at his watch. "I sort of have an appointment in a couple minutes," he said. "But what kind of file are we talking about?" he asked, sounding apprehensive.

"Let's say, a professor's secret file that held his exams?" Nancy suggested.

"Well, if I were trying to break through someone's password," he explained resignedly, "hypothetically speaking, of course—"

Nancy nodded firmly. "Of course."

"Then one general rule is that people will often use their birthday or wedding anniversary or a name that means a lot to them as their password. Which is pretty dumb, if you ask me, since they're so obvious."

Nancy thought to herself, Like a wife's name.

Andy looked around him, as if for a way out, then stood up. "Look, I've really gotta go," he said abruptly.

Nancy touched his arm for him to stay. "So okay," she pressed him, "once you know the password, how do you break in and actually steal information from someone else's computer? I mean, you're on your computer, and their computer is somewhere else. It's not like you can just hit a button, and presto, right?"

Andy nervously looked at his watch. "Look, guys, you're making me *really* late now. I gotta go." He stepped between their chairs, and then he was gone.

Reva wrinkled her nose in confusion. Nancy swallowed hard. Was Andy the one they were looking for?

If he was, there were tons of trouble ahead—for everybody.

"What was that all about?" Reva asked.

"I don't know," Nancy said worriedly, "but I hope it's not what I suspect."

Suspect? Reva wondered. Does she really think Andy could be behind this? Then again, he has been acting weird lately. And that stuff he was saying about money? Still, I just can't think of Andy as a thief. Or maybe I just won't.

Nancy turned toward the blank computer screen. "I guess I didn't find out that much, huh?"

"Well, tell me what you want to find out," Reva said. "Maybe I do know something."

"Okay," Nancy leaned back, her hands behind her head, thinking out loud. "The exam was stolen off Professor Ross's computer by someone outside, right? So it was someone on another computer."

Reva nodded. "I'm with you."

"And computers communicate by talking to each other through a phone line, right?"

Reva nodded. "Everyone in the Internet has an address, which is public information. Just like a phone book. So you can call another computer the way you call a friend, and you can talk to it—as long as you're not blocked by a password."

"The password," Nancy repeated. "How can you possibly find out someone's password?"

They thought a minute. "Well, if it's usually someone's birthday—" Reva said.

"Or a wife's name," Nancy finished the thought. "Which is what Ross said. But which name? There are thousands of them!"

Reva swiveled toward the computer. "I have an idea." She typed a few commands into the computer, and waited. "There you are," she said, as a screen labeled Hacker's Bulletin Board appeared.

"What's that?" Nancy asked, staring at the screen. As she leaned forward, her fingers accidentally grazed the Power On/Off button on the keyboard.

"Wait, don't touch that!" Reva said.

But it was too late—the computer bleeped once, then twice, then the screen went blank.

"Oops." Nancy blushed.

Reva cracked up. "Well, that *was* a giant party line, where computer hackers on the Internet from all over the world talk to one another."

"Can't we find it again?" Nancy asked.

Reva started typing. "Just stay away," Reva joked, "back there." She drew an imaginary line in the air about a foot away from the keyboard. "Okay," she murmured, "let's just post a question about our little problem and see what happens."

Reva typed: "Does anyone out there know anything about breaking passwords?" Then she typed her Internet address and sat back, her arms folded.

"Relax," Reva said. "This may take a while."

"Hey, look at that!" Nancy pointed at the screen.

Reva nodded with amazement. "That was fast."

A message had appeared: "Pieter Engel from Holland: I'm sending you a solution to your problem."

"Great!" Reva said excitedly.

"Holland," Nancy repeated, impressed.

A minute later she was copying Pieter Engel's "solution" into her account at Wilder. It was a program called Passbreak.

Reva scratched her head. "I've never heard of that before. Passbreak."

They thought a second.

"Passbreak," Nancy mumbled. "Break passwords!" She laughed. "It's a program for computer hackers to get into secret files."

"The only thing is," Reva said, squinting at the computer screen, "I don't know how it works. Let's play with this and see if we can figure it out." Reva bit her lip as she concentrated. "Let's set up a fake Internet address with a password. We'll use your name, *Nancy.*"

Nancy shifted in her chair. "And then break in with the program?"

"Exactly," Reva said, typing in one more command. "There—now we'll see."

They eagerly watched the monitor. Names by the hundreds scrolled up the screen.

"They're all female," Nancy said, amazed.

The program worked from the *A*'s through the *L*'s. Suddenly the computer screen froze on the name *Nancy,* drawing a box around it.

"Bingo!" Reva said proudly. "That's cool!"

"And in under a minute, too," Nancy muttered.

"Pretty easy."

Nancy nodded once. "Yeah. Way *too* easy."

Reva turned to Nancy. "Okay, so now what."

"So—" Nancy acted uncomfortable. "Does Andy have a program like that?"

Reva winced. *Nancy really does suspect him!* she realized. Then she checked herself. *Why am I protecting him?* she wondered. But she knew the answer. She liked him. She liked him a lot. She didn't think he was innocent, as much as she hoped he was.

"I don't think he has any programs like this one in his account," Reva said. "I'd know. I look through it all the time for the guide."

"Let's just see," Nancy said, reaching over Reva's hands and typing the right commands into the computer. Andy's Internet account appeared on the screen.

"How'd you know how to do that!" Reva gasped.

Nancy shrugged. "Quick learner?"

Reva glanced worriedly over her shoulder.

"Don't worry, I don't think he'll be back for a while," Nancy said.

"But how do you know?" Reva asked sadly.

"Just a hunch."

"I don't want to hurt him," Reva said. "I want to help him."

Nancy nodded at the computer. "Me, too. But the only way to help him is to do this. So let's go."

"Okay," Reva said uncertainly, and leaned in.

Andy's files floated up to the edge of the screen. Nancy pointed at each one, reciting it out loud. He had a file for each of his classes, a file called Letters & Stuff, a files called Dear Diary.

"Let's look at that," Reva said, only half-jokingly. Inwardly, she was hoping there'd be a diary entry about her.

"Reva!" Nancy said.

Reva smiled sheepishly. "Sorry, I know. It's private. But—uh-oh."

"Uh-oh's right," Nancy said, looking at the screen. "There's Passbreak."

"But how would he have broken the encryption code?" she asked, baffled.

Nancy shook her head. "I don't know—yet."

"Well, there's something I'd better tell you

now," Reva confessed reluctantly. "Andy's been saying some weird stuff about money lately. Like he really needs it badly, and quick."

Nancy tapped her chin. "That might explain it, or it might not. After all, whoever gave Ray a copy of that exam didn't ask for money, did he?"

"No," Reva said hopefully, suddenly cheered.

"On the other hand, whoever it is could be waiting to blackmail everyone who received a copy of the test. Or maybe this was just a freebee. The next exam wouldn't be so cheap." Nancy shook her head. "It's not adding up in Andy's favor—yet."

Reva stared sulkily at the screen. She pictured Andy's handsome face. She could still feel him poking her in the ribs and hear their playful laughter. The past few days with him he'd made her feel happy, *alive.*

"I can't believe it," she muttered under her breath. "Andy a computer thief? It just doesn't make sense."

Nancy sighed. "I know. But unfortunately, it might be starting to."

CHAPTER 10

No way!" Will cried, bolting out of the chair and pacing across the floor.

"Will!" George implored.

"I'm really sorry, you guys," Nancy said dejectedly. "Maybe I shouldn't have said anything until we were more sure."

The three of them were alone in the *Wilder Times* offices. It was late Thursday night.

Will was fuming. With his muscular arms folded across his chest, he peered intently across the room at Nancy. "Not only do I refuse to believe that my roommate could do anything like that," he said, "I wonder why you think you have the right to go around accusing people of cheating."

"Will!" George cried, coming to Nancy's defense. "Nancy would never say anything if she didn't believe it."

Will threw George a puzzled look. "Whose side are you on, anyway?"

I shouldn't have said anything, Nancy thought. I shouldn't have put them in this position.

But it was too late. The damage was done.

"Will, please," Nancy said. "I told you I'm not sure. It's only a suspicion—"

George was totally confused, and Nancy could tell she wanted to believe her, but was having a hard time. "Nan, you really believe Andy could be behind all this?"

Nancy shook her head. "Not yet—not totally. Actually, I was kind of hoping you might be able to tell me something that would clear him."

"What do you want me to say?" Will asked, accusing her.

"I want to help him," Nancy said for what she felt was the hundredth time. "So, maybe it's just a coincidence that he's been acting so weird lately?"

"He is under a lot of pressure," George said.

"From what?" Nancy wanted to know.

"I've been wondering that myself," Will cut in. "He just seems moodier lately. And he's been talking about money. But still, he definitely wouldn't do this."

George turned to Will, but she avoided his eyes. "Maybe Nancy's right. It does sort of add up."

She reached out to touch him, but Will didn't even notice her. His eyes narrowed. "So your theory seems pretty strong," he said to Nancy.

"But I still don't believe Andy did it. And I won't until you prove it."

George stood and went to him. Will enveloped her in his arms and planted a kiss on top of her head. They both turned to Nancy.

"Maybe we should all keep this to ourselves for a while," Nancy suggested. "Until we figure it out."

George nodded.

"What if you *can't* figure it out?" Will asked stubbornly.

Nancy shrugged, but she didn't say what she was thinking—that she'd have no choice.

"Okay," Will agreed reluctantly. "I won't say anything—yet. But I still refuse to believe Andy is mixed up in this stuff."

Peter tried to get a better view through the newspaper office window. He knew Nancy was in there. He'd seen her friend George and George's boyfriend, Will, enter a little while ago. He saw Nancy's head pass by the window, and his heart leaped—just a little, which was as much as he'd let it.

He'd been admiring the night sky while he waited, trying to catch any shooting stars, remembering his date with Nancy. They'd come here to stare at the sky and talk about nothing, just stuff. The rest of the world had vanished. Nancy had laughed and cracked jokes. She was irresistible.

But now he knew he had to tell her everything. The decision had been building in him all day.

The secrets and lying—not only to Nancy but to Jake—had totally occupied his brain. He'd sat all day in his room, tapping absently on his computer keyboard as the screen filled with question marks.

He knew he couldn't make a final decision about his secret until he knew what Nancy felt. But he had to tell her first. He was trapped, and he knew it.

"But don't count on any sympathy," he muttered under his breath, reminding himself for the thousandth time.

The outside door swung open. Peter crouched behind a bush. Wait a second, he thought, what are you hiding from? You may be irresponsible, but you're not a crook.

Still, the guilt kept him hidden there in the shadows, where he couldn't be seen.

He heard voices coming toward him and held his breath as George and Will walked by. They sounded upset. "I still can't believe it," he overheard George say.

"Don't," Will replied, "because it's not true."

They turned a corner, and Peter stood up. "That's strange," he said. "I hope Nancy's okay." He looked up at the office window with dread. The light was still on.

Taking a deep breath, he headed for the door. "Okay, Goodwin," he muttered. "Time to 'fess up."

He climbed the stairs slowly. "Strange," he

muttered at the office door. He'd expected the sound of typing, but all he heard was silence.

"Nancy?" he called, walking in.

She was sitting at her desk with her back to him. Her lamp was the only one in the office that was on, and she was surrounded by the light.

"Nancy," he said again.

Nancy turned around. "Peter!" she said, surprise showing on her face. Or was that sadness? Peter couldn't tell.

"Are you okay?" he asked.

Nancy smiled weakly. "Sure."

Peter took the seat next to hers and stared into her eyes. "I don't believe you."

"How are your mountains of work going?" she asked.

Peter could see she was still hurt.

"Not great," he said.

Peter could tell she knew something else was going on, something bigger.

"You've been avoiding me," Nancy said, not happily, but not angrily either.

"It's a long story," he said sadly.

"It had better be," Nancy retorted, half serious, and half poking fun.

They looked into each other's eyes. The corners of Nancy's mouth lifted in a sort of half-smile, and Peter's did, too. Then they both broke into relieved laughter.

"Well, I'm glad you're talking to me again," Nancy said, though Peter could see she was still troubled. "I mean, you *are* talking to me now, aren't you?"

Peter smiled. "That's why I'm here. I have something I want to say—"

Nancy's eyes locked onto his.

Peter had prepared a sort of speech, and he was racking his brain for a way to start while Nancy waited patiently.

Long seconds were passing. They were drifting closer. It was as if there were a magnetic field between them, pulling them together. The attraction was undeniable.

They were inches apart. Peter pushed aside a strand of hair from Nancy's face. But when he pulled his hand back, Nancy took it and held it gently. Then she moved in closer. Peter leaned in. Their eyes closed, and as if in a dream, they were kissing. It *was* a dream. At the touch of Nancy's soft lips, Peter felt his troubles lift out of him like water evaporating off a sidewalk after a rain.

Nancy, he thought, over and over and over. Nancy. It's real, it's real. . . .

His eyes flew open just as the office door slammed shut. They whirled around. A figure stepped out of the shadows and into the light.

Nancy gasped. "Dawn!"

CHAPTER 11

I finally have revenge, the hacker thought, listening with satisfaction to his computer hard drive whirring and clicking. He loved the sound computers made—as if they were thinking. As if they were human. Except they always did what they were told, and they didn't ask dumb questions or get suspicious.

He stared happily into his computer screen. "The damage is almost complete, Professor Ross. Your entire year and all your hard work is about to bomb."

He took in the sheaf of papers on his desk: all of Ross's plans for this semester and the next. Even some of his private research ideas—which he was sure some of the good professor's colleagues would love to see.

"It's a good thing you're so organized," he muttered. "The way you plan out an entire year at a time, all I have to do is pass out these labs and final exam questions, and the sabotage will be complete."

Then he focused on the information he had on the monitor: Top Secret: President's Report to the Board of Directors.

"It's like on-the-job training," he thought. "Thank you, Professor Ross. Because of you, I can now get any information I want. Information people might be willing to pay for."

Finally, that money! The thought of it relieved him.

"But information is valuable only when it's secret. I have to hurry...."

I can't get it out of my head, Reva thought to herself as she walked quickly across the quad back toward Thayer Hall. What was Andy doing with Passbreak in his files?

Hugging her books to her chest, she passed through the round pools of lamplight on the walkways. Her stomach gave a plaintive rumble. But what she wanted more than food was sleep. It had been a long day. Besides, sleep might be the only thing to keep her from thinking about Andy. The thought of him and that program—and his weird reactions to Nancy's questions—kept nagging at her.

"Hey there!" The voice came out of the dark. Footsteps fell in beside hers.

"Stuart?" Reva asked, wincing. She liked Stuart. He was amusing. But she didn't want conversation now. She wanted sleep.

"Aren't you afraid to be walking alone across the quad at this hour?" Stuart asked.

"Should I be?" Reva asked.

Stuart shrugged. "You never know, with all the ghosts and goblins around."

"Like you, for instance?"

"Nah, I'm harmless," Stuart said. "So, where are you going?"

Reva raised an eyebrow. Why is he being so nosy all of a sudden? she wondered.

"Where are *you* going, Stuart?"

Stuart seemed to falter, which made Reva really wonder what he was doing there.

"Waiting for you, of course," he said, grinning proudly.

Reva looked at him. "Tell me something: are you ever serious?"

Stuart stopped and snatched Reva's hand, sandwiching it between his. "About you, I am," he said, and fell to one knee. "Reva Ross, will you marry me?"

Rolling her eyes, Reva yanked her hand back and started walking away. "Sure, Stu," she said over her shoulder. "In about a million years."

Stuart caught up to her. "The truth is, I have a trig test tomorrow, and I was just taking a study break, on my way for a midnight pizza. Interested?"

"The only thing I'm interested in is saying hello to my pillow," Reva said, quickening her pace. "Besides, I've been in the computer lab all night."

"But I thought Andy and I finished up our work this afternoon," Stuart said.

Reva wondered whether she should let Stuart in on what was going on, then decided she should wait until she was sure. "I was just doing some personal stuff," Reva said evasively. "For my computer science class."

Stuart nodded. Reva thought he bought it. "So can I go now?"

Stuart didn't move. He had something on his mind. "Andy sure seems distracted lately, huh?"

Does he already know something? Reva wondered, peering at him in the half-light. She couldn't be certain. The only thing she *was* certain about was the fact that she was exhausted.

Reva shrugged and smiled groggily. "I guess," she replied. "But it's just normal stuff. Tests, homework—you know."

Stuart seemed lost in thought for a second, then snapped out of it. "Yeah." He smiled. "I understand."

"See you tomorrow," Reva said, walking away.

"In the lab?" he called out.

"Okay," she said.

"What time?"

Reva pretended not to hear. She had a feeling that their work on the Internet Guide was going to stop for a while, if not for good.

"I'm really sorry," Dawn was saying earnestly over and over. "I knew I shouldn't have come. I

131

just wanted to talk to you, Nancy. But I saw Peter heading in the same direction, and I—"

"You followed me?" Peter asked, shocked.

Nancy could hardly look Dawn in the eyes. She felt embarrassed and guilty that Dawn had caught her and Peter together—and in the middle of a passionate kiss.

"No, *I'm* sorry," Nancy said, realizing that Dawn and Peter still hadn't worked things out. Besides, what was she doing getting involved with someone after just breaking up with Ned? Her mind was a jumble of regrets.

Everyone seemed too embarrassed to talk. Nancy respected and admired Dawn, and obviously, Dawn still had strong feelings for Peter.

"I think *I'm* the one who should really be sorry here," Peter finally spoke up.

Dawn nodded her agreement.

"You wanted to talk to me?" Nancy asked her. But Dawn seemed unreachable. She was glaring at Peter.

The discomfort was almost impossible to take.

"I think I'd better say something here," Peter said, obviously struggling for words.

"I think you'd better," Dawn said, her eyes wet.

Peter looked at Nancy. "There's something about me you don't know."

Dawn looked at Nancy in surprise. "You mean he didn't tell you yet?"

"Tell me what?" Nancy asked. Now she was really confused.

Dawn took a step toward Peter. "I can't believe you didn't tell her," she said bitterly. "How could you get involved with someone else so soon, after what you told me—"

"It was more than that, Dawn!" Peter cut her off. "I liked you, but—but, I just didn't love you."

Dawn didn't seem fazed. "You're so confused you couldn't really love anyone right now—except yourself maybe."

Nancy looked back and forth between them. There was something else going on. Something bigger than their breakup.

"How could you do it, Peter?" Dawn went on. "How could you get involved with Nancy right after you broke up with me? You told me you needed to be alone to figure out your life." Dawn's voice rose with anger. "How could you—when you have a child with another woman!"

Nancy's knees felt weak. Dawn was shaking with rage and hurt. "And when *I* still love *you!*" she said.

Dawn whirled around and headed for the door, sobbing.

"Dawn!" Nancy called after her.

"Let her go," Peter said quietly.

Nancy ran for the door, but by the time she got there, Dawn was gone.

Nancy's mind was reeling. Another woman? Child? What was Dawn talking about?

When she returned to the office, Peter was sitting in a chair, his head in his hands.

"I guess I owe you an explanation," he said.

Nancy sat beside him.

Peter cleared his throat. "When I was in high school, I had a girlfriend, Anna," he began. "We liked each other, but I was accepted here for college, and she was going to school in California, so we said we'd see what happened with our relationship. After a couple of weeks she met someone, and so did I." He shrugged. "Our breakup was unavoidable. We stayed friends, but grew apart."

"Like Ned and me," Nancy said.

Peter nodded. "Except that we weren't as serious. Anyway, after freshman year, I went home to visit my parents before my summer job started and ran into Anna. She was home for just a few days before she went back to California for her summer job. We were old friends and got together for dinner. We had fun. We laughed at the way we had been. We talked about who we'd met. I was happy for her. Neither of us was seeing anyone at that time."

Peter took a big breath. "We went for a walk to our old hangout, a cliff that overlooked the whole town. I guess it was corny, but in high school we thought it was pretty cool."

Peter swallowed hard. Nancy had to lean in to hear him. "I guess ... I don't know," he continued. "It was a beautiful night, she was going back to California the next morning, and it was nice not to think about anything. It was like for old times' sake. Am I making any sense?"

Nancy nodded knowingly. "I get the picture."

"It was only one night," Peter said. "But we were so stupid! I can't believe how irresponsible we were!"

Nancy didn't respond.

Peter sighed. "Anna got pregnant. She called me here at school with the news, and we decided to tell our parents all together. There was a big conference, the six of us around my parents' dining room table. Everyone took it really well."

"What did you do?" Nancy prodded.

"We talked about giving the baby up for adoption after it was born. My parents even offered to adopt it and bring it up. But Anna said that on the plane home, she'd decided she wanted to keep the baby. She dropped out of school in California and took night classes at a community college near home."

Peter raised his eyes. "We have a son," he said. "He was born last March fifteenth. His name is Ben."

At first Nancy was speechless. The whole story seemed incredibly sad. But then she remembered the flicker of pride in Peter's eyes when he mentioned his son's name. It took a minute to sink in. Peter was a father!

She took his hand. It was cold and damp. She was overwhelmed with a riot of emotions. She was sad that Peter was trapped and angry that he hadn't told her, but still very attracted to him.

"You're mad," Peter said. "I can tell."

"Well, yes. No." Nancy shook her head. "I don't know, maybe just confused."

Peter laughed grimly. "Me, too."

"Why didn't you marry her?" Nancy asked. Though she hoped she already knew the answer.

Peter shook his head. "We never considered it. We liked each other, but we weren't in love."

"And Dawn?" Nancy probed fearfully, afraid that he might still have feelings for Dawn.

Peter sighed. "We started seeing each other at the end of last year. I was lonely. I liked her a lot, but I'd been a father only a couple months and wanted to take things slow. I was talking to Anna every night about Ben. I wanted to hear everything about him, every time he made some dumb little noise. So I had secrets from Dawn from the beginning. I knew it wouldn't work. I was going to let things cool off during the summer. But—"

"She was already in love with you," Nancy finished the thought.

Peter smiled sadly.

"Wow," Nancy said, overwhelmed. Then something struck her. "Does Jake know?"

Peter shook his head. "I couldn't tell him. It's the only secret between us. Only Dawn knows— and now you."

Nancy sat back wearily—she was also relieved. Everything was out in the open. Not that it made things any easier.

Nancy slowly raised her eyes. "And me?" she asked tentatively. "Where do I fit in?"

"That's where it gets really confusing," Peter replied, squeezing her hand. "Because I . . . well, I *really* like you. I think I even . . ."

Nancy put a finger to his lips. She didn't want him to say it unless he really meant it. Unless he'd he able to say it again.

Peter took her hand away. "I might love you," he said, gazing into her face.

Her eyes moist, Nancy held her breath. The words "I love you, too" rose to her lips, but she held them back. She had the urge to embrace him and kiss him, and hold him until all his problems vanished.

What would it be like being involved with someone who's already a father? she thought. Am I ready for the responsibility of what could happen if we became serious?

Then an overwhelming thought shadowed everything: I'm too young for this.

Yet, Nancy couldn't deny that part of her didn't want anything to change.

But it's already changed, Nancy realized.

"What are you going to do?" she asked quietly.

"I came here to tell you I'm going home tomorrow—"

Nancy held her breath.

"Just for the day," Peter added quickly. "To talk to Anna and see Ben."

Nancy nodded. She swallowed her fear. He had to do what he had to do. But would he come back?

"Okay," she said. "But what about Dawn?"

"I'll try to talk to her tonight." Peter stood. "I'd better go."

Nancy pushed herself up. "Thanks," she said.

"For what?" Peter asked, truly surprised.

"For being honest and telling me everything. I'm sure you'll do the right thing—whatever it is."

Somehow, the total honesty made them both unafraid. They stared openly into each other's eyes. In the back of her mind, Nancy thought that it might be for the last time.

"Can I give you a hug?" Peter asked.

"You don't have to ask," Nancy said.

Wrapped in his arms, Nancy rested her hands on Peter's strong back, trying to memorize the feel of him. On the verge of tears, she had the urge to kiss him. But she stepped back and let him go.

"I'll call you when I get back," Peter said. He turned and disappeared through the door.

Nancy sat at her little cubicle, listening for the sound of the outside door closing. As Peter's footsteps hurried away, she thought wistfully of her own life.

All this talk about the past made her nostalgic for Ned. She probed her heart, which used to beat furiously at the thought of him. But when she tried to remember the touch of his mouth on hers, she couldn't. With every day that passed, it was getting harder and harder to picture Ned in her mind.

Nancy thought of their relationship as a fire that had burned itself out. Her feelings for Ned now were like embers, cooled to the edge of extinction.

Her thoughts returned to Peter. What was he going to do? she wondered, knowing she could supply the answer. She'd spotted it in his eyes. That was one of the things she loved most about Peter. His eyes were like windows. And tonight, she was sure, the windows were closing on her.

CHAPTER 12

As Bess hustled across campus toward Java Joe's, she slid her eyes surreptitiously from side to side. She had her Kappa radar up. In the event of a Soozie Beckerman spotting she had a new plan: run away!

She didn't know what wickedly dumb thing Soozie had in mind for the freshmen plebes next, but she wasn't going to hang around, waiting to find out. Nancy had called a mandatory "update hour" with George and her: Java Joe's, 9 A.M.

She couldn't wait to find out what was going on with Ginny and the cheating scandal. She'd been so involved with her Kappa responsibilities and *Grease!* rehearsals and classes that she'd almost lost track of it.

All three of them descended on the coffee bar at exactly the same time.

"Latte, extra sugar," Bess said.

"I'll have a latte, too," Nancy told the guy behind the counter.

"Do you have *triple* espresso?" George asked, slapping her book bag down on the counter.

"Okay, Nan," Bess said as they slid into a booth. "We're all ears."

Nancy stared thirstily into her latte. "I need some of this before I talk."

Bess turned expectantly to George, who shook her head. "Don't look at me. You first."

"Well," Bess began, "the Kappas are totally destroying my social life. Casey Fontaine thinks I'm the most infantile human being to walk the earth, and people snicker at me when I go into my classes. I can't walk across the quad without entire crowds erupting in laughter, and my hair is permanently flat from carrying a textbook on my head. Other than that, everything's perfect!"

Nancy and George burst into laughter.

Bess blushed. "It's great to have supportive friends."

Nancy and George only laughed harder.

"Maybe I'll join *that* table," Bess said, nodding at a huge-looking jock with a buzz cut and tattoos on both arms. "He looks more welcoming."

"Look, Bess," Nancy said, "just lighten up a little. All that pledging stuff is so goofy it's funny."

George chimed in, "You see the humor, don't you?"

"For other people, maybe," Bess said. Then she tried to think about it from someone else's point of view. "I guess it is kind of funny," she said tentatively.

"*Kind* of funny?" George said. "It's *very* funny."

"Besides"—Nancy put her hand on Bess's shoulder—"it'll all be over soon. And next year, you'll be able to do the same thing to the new freshmen."

Bess rubbed her palms together. "I see your point." She downed her coffee.

"So," George said, expecting Nancy to speak next.

Nancy tried to smile, but settled for a small shrug.

"Is anything wrong?" Bess asked.

"Peter dropped a big piece of news last night," Nancy said quietly.

Bess gasped. "He asked you to marry him!"

George rolled her eyes. "Bess, look at Nancy. Does she look like a woman who was just proposed to?"

George was right, Bess knew. Nancy looked anything but happy.

"He didn't ask me to marry him," Nancy said, "but it looks like things are breaking off before they have a chance to start."

"But he already kissed you!" Bess interjected.

George shook her head. "You know that a kiss doesn't have to mean anything," she said.

"You're right," Bess answered. "But Peter seemed different. He seemed sincere. He seemed—"

Nancy cut Bess off. "He's a father."

Bess looked at George. George looked at Nancy. "Sorry, what did you say?" Bess asked.

"He has a son with his old girlfriend from high school," Nancy explained. "But you can't tell anyone. It's a major secret."

Bess couldn't hide her shock.

"Um, Bess, do you mind picking your jaw up off the table?" George whispered.

"Actually, that was my reaction, too," Nancy said. "He's going home today to talk to Anna—that's her name—about the whole situation."

George whistled. "That's about the last thing I expected you to tell us."

"It was the last thing I expected to hear," Nancy said. "But I knew something was bothering him because the minute we started getting close, he backed away.

"Anyway," Nancy continued, taking a big breath, "that's it for me. I just wanted you guys to know as my two best friends on the planet. I'm sure I'll have an update in a day or two."

George touched her hand. "I'm really sorry."

Nancy tried to smile. "Thanks."

"You like him a lot?" Bess asked gently.

Nancy nodded. "A *lot*. But let's talk about something else now."

"No problem," Bess said. "How about Ginny?"

"Hold on to your seats," Nancy warned, then told Bess what she suspected about Andy and how easily she and Reva had broken through a password. "It's this encryption stuff that we're not sure about," she said uncertainly.

Bess gasped, turning to George. "I don't believe it! Andy?"

George could only nod. "I didn't believe it either. In fact, I still don't. I'm positive Andy's innocent. I just wish we could prove it. Will was so upset last night that he'd hardly talk to me, and it could hurt our relationship. Clearing Andy would put things back on track for us."

Bess was overwhelmed. *If I wasn't so focused on my own stuff, I would have known all this,* she chided herself. *First Nancy, now this. I could have helped.*

"I haven't been there for you guys," she said apologetically. "It's like I'm hardly part of your lives anymore."

"Don't worry, Bess," Nancy said. "You're the best friend anyone could have. I *am* trying to help Andy," she said to George. "But it's hard. I don't know that much about computers—"

Bess held her breath as she detected the tension between her two best friends. She couldn't remember the last time they'd even had a squabble.

George put down her empty espresso glass. "Can you use me?" she asked straightforwardly.

"But you have a class," Nancy reminded her.

"I'll blow it off," George said decidedly. "This is more important. And it's Friday. Half the class won't show up anyway."

Bess sunk into her chair. She wanted to help,

too. "I have rehearsal today," she mumbled, "but I guess I can skip it—"

"You don't need to," Nancy reminded her. "I know how important the show is to you. Besides, we'll be all right."

"This place is really quiet," George whispered as she followed Nancy through room after room of the underground computer lab. Most of the terminals were occupied.

Nancy had more than the computer thefts on her mind. More than Andy's future or George and Will. Or Ginny and Ray.

She was still thinking about Peter. She pictured him driving home, picking up his little son and kissing him, changing his diapers. At first, the thought warmed her, but then it made her realize that she and Peter had never really had a chance. There was too much standing between them. Their relationship had been doomed from the start.

When Nancy and George reached the last room, only one of the terminals was occupied. A figure sat slumped over the keyboard, empty coffee cups at her feet.

"Reva." Nancy gently shook her shoulder.

Reva started awake. "What! Who?" Then she saw Nancy and George and rubbed her eyes. Reva's hair was messy, and she was wearing the same jeans and the wrinkled shirt from the night before.

"Have you been here all night?" George asked as she and Nancy pulled up chairs.

"Not all. I went home, but I couldn't sleep, so I came back and logged onto the Hacker's Bulletin Board on the Internet to see what I could find out about passwords and raiding computer files. I exchanged messages with some guy in Germany, another in Indiana, one girl in New York City."

"And?" George asked anxiously.

Reva dug through a stack of notes. "I found out that when someone breaks into someone else's computer files, there's usually evidence. Like 'ghost files.' "

"Or like fingerprints?" Nancy asked.

"Exactly," Reva confirmed. "The best part is that you can trace these 'prints' if someone breaks into a particular file a lot."

"And whoever it is would have had to break into Ross's file a lot, right?" Nancy inquired hopefully.

Reva nodded. "Let's hope so."

"So did you try it?" Nancy asked.

Reva smiled weakly. "You have to have a special program."

Nancy focused on Reva expectantly. She finally nodded. "I got it from the girl in New York, but I was waiting for you to try it. I was afraid of what I'd find."

"Okay," Nancy said resolutely. "Now that we're all here—let's do it."

"Here we go," Reva said, typing in the commands to start the program.

It was like watching a game, with the score tied and seconds to go. It was that same feeling of suspense—but instead of excitement, there was only anxiety.

The computer stopped churning. A message flashed on the screen that Nancy didn't understand. Reva was nodding, though. "There's a ghost file attached to Ross's account," she declared, smiling.

"Whose is it?" George asked eagerly.

Nancy pointed at the screen. "It gave a seven-digit number. A phone number?" Nancy asked.

Reva nodded. "That's what one of those guys said last night. We'd either get a phone number, which we could trace, or an encrypted code number, which we couldn't."

None of them said a thing. They'd been looking for this number, but also dreaded finding it. If it was a phone number, and it was Andy's, then Reva and George should know it.

Nancy cleared her throat. "So—does either of you recognize the number?"

Neither Reva nor George replied, and Nancy's heart sank. They don't want to say, she feared.

Then she saw the glints in their eyes.

Reva shook her head. "I don't recognize it, do you, George?"

George was grinning from ear to ear. "It's not Andy and Will's phone number. Doesn't that prove something?"

Nancy was glad, but she didn't want to get too excited. "The only thing it proves is that he

147

wasn't using a computer from his apartment. But it helps—a lot."

Reva looked Nancy straight in the eye. "I think we should get Andy down here. Now."

George was nodding vigorously. "Me, too."

"We'll ask him to help us trace the number and see how he reacts—" Nancy said.

"But where is he?" George lamented.

Reva's eyes widened as she peered into the screen. Numbers were changing, and file names were disappearing. Fast.

"Andy's here!" Reva cried. "He's somewhere in the computer lab!"

"How do you know?" Nancy asked, leaning over the screen.

"Wait, don't touch that!" Reva said.

Nancy had pressed a button, and the screen went haywire.

"Nancy!" Reva groaned.

Nancy reddened. "Sorry—did I goof it up again?"

Reva typed a couple of commands, and the screen returned to normal. "Keep her away from here, will you, George? She's dangerous. . . . Wait! There goes another one. Andy's changing files!"

"But how do you know he's here?" Nancy repeated.

"See that ID number in the upper right-hand corner? That's like the address of the user."

George peeked over her shoulder. "And he's

right here? In one of the rooms of the computer lab?"

"Not only that—he's changing files in our Internet account!" Reva cried. "Wait a second—oh no! He just erased one!"

"Which way?" George shouted, racing with Reva and Nancy through the computer lab. She was really worried. If Andy was innocent, why would he have been moving those files? Why would he have been erasing them?

George slowed as Reva and Nancy cruised ahead. She paused to think behind some guy slumped over his keyboard with a San Diego Padre hat yanked down over his head. He was typing madly.

Wait—San Diego? Andy's from San Diego! The Padres are his favorite team.

George stepped behind him and squinted at his monitor. It was all just numbers and weird names to her. "Hi, Andy," she said.

The fingers on the keyboard froze. George could see the reflection of Andy's face in the screen.

"We've been looking for you."

"Why?" Andy snapped.

Nancy and Reva were doubling back. "Look who I found," George said.

Reva peered into the screen. "Andy, what are you doing to our Internet account?"

Andy's face went white. George felt a lump in her throat. The Andy she knew was happy-go-lucky and funny and seductively handsome. This Andy was serious and bothered—and trapped.

"Why are you checking up on me?" Andy asked.

"We have something to ask you," Nancy said simply.

George cut in. "Do you know anything about the cheating scandal?" she asked him point blank.

"Sure, I guess," he said vaguely. "The same stuff you know—"

"What George wants to know," Nancy said, "is if you know more about it than you should."

Andy took off his cap and raked his fingers through his straight, dark hair. He bowed his head and sighed, and George's hopes of his innocence evaporated. "Andy," she said, and shook her head sadly.

"I can't believe it," Reva lamented.

"Why did you do it?" George asked.

"Do what?" Andy asked innocently.

"Break into Professor Ross's files," Nancy said, keeping her voice low so no one else could hear.

Andy was obviously confused. He glanced at his computer monitor, then at Nancy, Reva, and George in turn. "Wait a second. You think *I* stole that exam?"

"Didn't you?" George asked.

Andy was horrified. "No!"

George was beginning to get excited. "Really?"

Reva was breathless. "You're sure?"

"No! I mean, *yes,* I'm sure!" Andy looked as if half of him wanted to laugh and half wanted to scream. "You mean you think *I'm* the hacker?"

"Then what are you doing now?" Nancy asked, nodding toward the screen.

Andy glanced left and right at the other students, who were throwing them annoyed glances. "I can't talk here," he said mysteriously. "Let's go to the back of the room."

They followed Andy in silence.

"Okay," Andy said, lowering himself in front of his and Reva's usual terminal. "I shouldn't tell you this because it's all top secret. It can't leave this room. Agreed?"

Everyone nodded anxiously.

"Just after Reva and I started working on the Internet Guide," Andy began, "someone in the university president's office asked me to put together a top secret computer system that would protect the school's files from hackers. Like an alarm system for a house."

There were a few seconds of stunned silence.

"That's it?" George asked.

Andy shrugged. "That's it."

"Why didn't you tell me?" Reva asked, obviously hurt.

"It wasn't an option," Andy said apologetically. "They said I had to keep it secret. If I told you, maybe you would have accidentally said something to Will, or even Stuart."

"But what about that weird stuff in your account?" Nancy asked. "Like the Passbreak file?"

Andy nodded. "Okay. So I'm setting up the system. But how am I supposed to know it works?"

A glint of understanding came to Nancy's eyes. "By posing as a hacker," she proposed.

"Exactly!" Andy replied.

"You're testing the system," Reva said.

"I have to try every which way to break in. And then I have to try to break the encryption codes. If you read the files on the screen, you won't be able to make sense of them. They're all in a code that I made up. Only the university president will have the program to break it."

Nancy was waiting. "So—does it work?"

Andy grinned proudly. "So far."

George was giddy with happiness. So was Reva. She leaned over and planted a big kiss on Andy's cheek, then cleared her throat. Everyone was laughing. George clamped Andy in a tight bear hug. "I have to tell Will," she said breathlessly.

Andy eyed her. "Will? You mean *he* suspected me too?"

"No," Nancy interjected. "He never thought you'd be involved. But Reva said you'd been talking a lot about money, so I asked him—"

Andy was laughing to himself.

"Don't be mad at me," Reva said.

"I'm not mad at you." He shook his head. "I've been totally obsessed with money."

"But why?" George said.

"I was hoping to buy a totally hot computer

system, but it costs a lot of money. That's one of the reasons I took on this job. With the salary from the password project, and the Internet Guide, I had an idea of starting a consulting business. You know, help everyone get logged on to the Internet, answer their questions. But I'm sick of this dungeon," he said, waving at the bare, dingy room. "I wanted to do it from my apartment."

Reva was bouncing excitedly in her seat, George thought she was ready to launch herself—and she did. Landing right around Andy's neck!

"I was so worried," she said.

Andy held her tight. "It's okay," he said.

George cleared her throat. "We still have business to do, guys."

Nancy nodded. "Andy, I'm really sorry for having suspected you, but—"

Andy held up a hand. "I understand. You had no choice. As weird as I've been acting, I would have suspected me, too."

"We'll have to celebrate later," Nancy said insistently. "After we know who the real hacker is."

Andy rolled up his sleeves and turned on the computer, all business. "This person is really starting to get under my skin. Tell me everything you know."

Nancy and Reva explained to Andy all the information they'd gathered. "Now we have a ghost file number that might be a phone number but might not," Reva said.

"What is it?" Andy asked.

"Seven-nine-seven-four-six-three-six," Reva recited, reading off her notes.

Andy started typing furiously.

George leaned in, fascinated by the codes appearing on the screen. "What are you doing?"

Andy winked at her. "It's better if you don't know."

He typed in a couple of different commands, then leaned back. "Voilà," he said, and they all watched as phone numbers by the dozens started floating up the screen.

CHAPTER 13

Andy watched his monitor intently as it filled with more information after he had typed in the ghost file number.

"It's a phone number, and it *does* belong to a Wilder student," he said as the computer spat out its confirmation.

"Who?" Nancy asked.

"Wait," Andy said, "it's like cracking a lock combination—one digit at a time."

"Off-campus housing," George said as the address 60 Waterman Street appeared.

"That's near the building where Will and I live!" Andy cried. "That huge, old Victorian house."

"He's a sophomore," Nancy said, pointing at the graduation date.

Then the name appeared.

No one said a word. They stared at the screen.

"I don't believe it," Reva moaned.

Andy felt his anger catch fire in his throat. "Stuart O'Brien!" he said, seething. "I'll kill him!"

"Not unless I kill him first," Reva added. "But I have to hand it to him. He's smarter than we all thought."

"Yeah," Andy said, furious. "The jerk was probably spying on me, stealing my secret project piece by piece. I can't believe he was working with me all this time, and I didn't even know what he was doing."

Reva was still shaking her head in disbelief. "Stuart got away with all this."

"Unfortunately, he *still* might get away with it," Nancy said. "We'll need more proof. The phone trace might not be enough to positively link him to the stealing of Professor Ross's exam files. We could also use some hard evidence."

Nancy was grinning mischievously. "You're a pretty good hacker yourself, aren't you, Andy?"

He knew what she as getting at. "You want me to break into Stuart's personal files?"

"It would serve him right," Reva murmured.

"I don't know," Andy hedged. "The university gave me access to all this stuff for the project. I'd be abusing the privilege."

"You'd be stopping Stuart from probably doing a lot more. Who knows what other files he's had access to," Nancy pointed out. "And you'd be helping Ginny Yuen."

"Come on, Andy!" Reva urged him. "This is

no time to be a goody-goody. Stuart deserves to be caught; he's committing a crime."

"Okay, okay," Andy said, fending them off. "I guess rules are meant to be broken sometimes."

He started up the Passbreak program to crack Stuart's account. He tried female names, then male names. Nothing. He tried dates. Still nothing.

George and Reva started to grumble.

"Don't give up yet," Andy murmured. "There's one more possibility—" He sat back and waited. The computer hummed, then stopped.

"Robin Hood?" they all said in unison as Stuart's password appeared on the screen.

George wrinkled her nose. "I don't get it."

"Open up his directory," Reva suggested.

Andy nodded and did it. "Uh-oh."

Reva pointed at the screen. Files were vanishing, one blip at a time.

"He knows we're here," Nancy murmured.

"He's erasing all the evidence!" Andy cried.

Nancy shot out of her chair. "Let's go. We're running out of time!"

Andy led the others to the old Victorian on Waterman Street.

"There he is," Nancy said, pointing to Stuart's name on the directory. He lived on the top floor. "But the front door's locked."

They all peered in the front windows of the ground floor apartments, trying to get someone's attention, but no one was home. They waited on the steps, watching the door anxiously. Suddenly it opened, and an unsuspecting guy walked out with his nose deep in a book. Andy grabbed the door before it closed, and the group sprinted for the stairs.

There was one door at the very top. Andy walked right up to the door and pounded on it with his fist. "Stuart! Open up!"

Nancy held up a hairpin. "Just because he won't let us in doesn't mean we can't make ourselves at home."

"But isn't that illegal?" Reva asked.

Andy snorted. "What's he going to do, turn us in?"

Nancy worked the lock, and the door clicked open. Inside, she flipped on the light. Stuart didn't have much furniture: a bed, a desk, a chair, a small refrigerator. The room was filled with books, magazines, and newspapers.

"I wonder where he went? He must have just been here—his computer is still warm," Andy said after pulling a bedsheet off a brand-new, topflight computer system. "Look at this. It's as nice as anything the university has." Andy eyed it enviously.

"Look around," Nancy said. "Look for anything."

"I'll get on the computer and see what's there," Andy offered.

Nancy, George, and Reva began to check out

the room. "Nothing under his bed," Reva called out.

"I can't find anything in his desk," George added.

Andy turned away from the computer, dejected. "He erased everything."

Nancy was standing in the middle of the room. "But there should be paper evidence," she said. "He handed out printed copies of that exam. If I were Stuart, where would I hide it?"

"I wouldn't hold on to anything," Andy suggested.

Nancy nodded. "Right. So maybe he forgot something. Maybe he left a copy lying around."

She scanned the small room. A copy of Monday morning's *Wilder Times* lay on the desk. She picked it up. Stuart had underlined a few paragraphs of Jake's article.

"Thanks, Jake," she muttered. "Maybe you gave Stuart some new ideas."

Nancy stared at a pile of computer books and newspapers in the far corner of the room. "What's that?" She walked over and lifted off a stack of books. "Maybe in here," she said excitedly, yanking open the top drawer of a metal filing cabinet that had been almost hidden under the stack.

Andy, Reva, and George gathered around her, and they started thumbing through the labeled folders. Suddenly Nancy spotted an unlabeled folder, hidden inside another folder. She pulled it out and started leafing through the sheets of paper inside.

"Yes!" she cried, holding up a single piece of paper.

Reva squinted at it. "What does it say? Is it a copy of the exam?"

"It's better," Nancy said. "It says, 'Biology 215, Professor Ross, Final Exam.' "

"Bingo," Andy said, snatching it from her hands.

"There are already a bunch of copies of the other test floating around campus," Nancy said. "But he couldn't have a copy of the final exam, unless—"

"Unless he stole it from the professor's computer," George finished the thought.

"Look, there's more," Nancy said, checking other sheets in the folder. "There seem to be some of Professor Ross's personal research notes and his plans for next semester."

"So where is Stuart now?" Reva wondered aloud.

"Back in the computer lab," Andy declared, pointing at the user address on the screen. "He's at it again."

Ginny drew back from Ray, the warm taste of his kiss still on her tongue. They were in a dark corner of the Underground, and since it was daytime, there wasn't much activity. Just a few people eating sandwiches and chips. The stage was empty. Ray had brought his guitar along. Maybe he could get some practice in, try out a few new tunes.

I love you, Ginny thought, gazing into his seductive eyes. But she couldn't say it out loud yet. She knew it was too soon, and there was too much going on. The second their lips parted, thoughts of her problems flooded back in.

"When are they going to find the hacker?" Ginny moaned.

"We all know it wasn't you," Ray said lovingly. "Don't worry so much."

"But I still don't have my work-study job back."

"It'll be okay," Ray assured her.

Ginny had an idea to occupy them. "When this is cleared up, they'll probably give the test over again. Maybe you should study some more. I'll help."

Ray laughed at her. "I know that my grade on the test is real. I did well. If I have to take it again, I'll take it again. But I'm happy with the way I did. Besides"—he took her in his arms— "you're always tutoring me. Maybe I can tutor you a little. Here—" He handed her his guitar and spaced her fingers over the strings. "Now strum."

Ginny fanned her fingers over the strings. A sort-of chord came out.

"Beautiful!" Ray cried. "Now do this." He showed her how to change the chord. "Okay, now every time I nod, change to the next chord. Ready?"

Ginny looked around the Underground. "Okay," she said, and shrugged.

Ray started to sing a well-known lyrical ballad as Ginny played along, mouthing the words silently to herself.

Eyes closed, Ray lifted his voice. Ginny began to feel the music in her hands. She felt the rhythm of his voice. She played as he sang.

"I love you," she murmured, barely a whisper. But, singing, he couldn't hear her.

Stuart was grinning from ear to ear. "Hi, everybody!"

Andy stepped forward with his fists clenched, but Reva tugged him by the back of his shirt.

Everyone in the computer room was watching them.

"I thought you didn't know anything about computers," Andy said accusingly.

Stuart winked. "You're a great teacher."

Nancy laughed ruefully. "I have to hand it to you, Stuart, you're pretty smart."

"But not smart enough," Andy said.

Stuart smiled. "I just deleted the last file. That's the beauty of computers. Evidence vanishes—poof!—without a trace."

"Then there's no reason not to let us in on your little plan," Nancy said. "Since there's no evidence, of course."

Andy started to say something, but Nancy grabbed his hand and squeezed it, and he closed his mouth. Stuart seemed to think a second, then shrugged. "Sure, why not?" he said with a hint of pride in his voice.

"I was in Professor Ross's advanced seminar on molecular biology last year," Stuart began, "and he flunked me."

Nancy noticed Stuart's expression change as he started to talk about Professor Ross. He seemed to be getting angry.

"He doesn't care who he flunks. He doesn't care if his students' parents don't talk to them for weeks or tell them what failures they are." Stuart's voice began to rise, and his face was turning red. "He doesn't care about people. Only about his research." Stuart was almost yelling now. He stopped speaking, as he noticed their stunned expressions.

"And so"—he smiled at them all, composing himself—"I thought I'd pay him back. I'm the first computer Robin Hood. I took from the powerful and gave to the needy."

"And took from the needy, too," Andy couldn't help saying.

Stuart acted surprised. "But you're all students like me. Ross doesn't care about you. Why should you care about him?"

"Who do you think you are!" Nancy blurted out in exasperation. "Ginny lost her job and is about to be expelled. Andy was almost falsely accused. And now Ross is going to flunk his whole class on this test. All because of you! That's what you call giving to the needy?"

She saw that Stuart had lost his smile. For a moment, at least, he appeared to be embarrassed.

"Oh, well. See what happens when you try to help? Maybe next time." Stuart gave a half-shrug.

"There won't be a next time," Nancy said.

She caught a glint of panic in Stuart's eye. He glanced at the computer screen, which was still blank. "There's no evidence," he said smugly.

Nancy held up the papers she had taken from Stuart's file. "Except these," she said. "I'm sure the campus administration and Professor Ross will want to know how you managed to have copies of the professor's final exam and personal research notes."

Stuart's face went white. Defeated, he sat down in front of the computer and put his head in his hands.

"It's so funny," George mused out loud. "With all this incredible technology and fancy equipment, a couple pieces of paper solve the case."

Peter poked his head into the newspaper office. He was still stiff from his car ride back to Wilder. His hands were shaking. He realized he was more nervous than he thought. He'd left very early to get back to campus. Somehow he felt out of place, as if he didn't belong.

It was a perfect Saturday morning in fall. The sky was clear and the air warm. Everyone seemed to be outside having fun—everyone but him.

He visualized Nancy in her cubicle at the newspaper office. He could hear her laughter ringing out. When he'd left her Thursday night, she'd been speechless and near tears. He hadn't stopped thinking about her since. Those few seconds they had to kiss—then Dawn interrupting.

He knew he wanted Nancy then, but he needed her now—needed her to understand.

"Nancy?" he called quietly as he walked into the office. But as he peeked over the partition, his heart sank. Every cell of his body felt sadness and regret.

Nancy and Jake were sitting shoulder to shoulder, their heads inches apart in front of Nancy's computer. They looked as if they were putting the finishing touches on an article. He saw the headline at the top of the screen: "W.U. Hacker Nabbed at His Own Game."

Peter arranged a strained smile on his face. "So you got him."

Nancy and Jake whirled around at once. "Pete! Where have you been?" Jake said enthusiastically.

Nancy smiled tentatively. He could see she was waiting to hear his news.

"Lots of excitement around here," Jake said, slapping Peter on the shoulder. "It was Stuart O'Brien!"

"Stuart?" Peter asked, confused.

"I'll explain later," Jake said, words flowing out of his mouth faster than he could handle. "But Professor Ross is setting another exam for next week. Everyone will have a second chance.

And all because of her!" Jake was grinning at Nancy.

"And my friends," Nancy added, blushing. "I didn't do it alone."

"That's great. Say, can I talk to you a minute?" Peter asked her.

Confusion crossed Jake's eyes. Peter expected that. He knew Jake liked Nancy, but he'd worry about him later.

"In private?" Peter added.

Jake looked from Nancy to Peter and back again. "No problem," he said after a second, still puzzled. "I think I'll run and get a cup of coffee." He loped out of the office.

Peter took his seat. Nancy looked at him, waiting.

"I talked things over with Anna," he began. "On the way home, I'd actually decided to drop out of school and get a job so I could be near her and Ben."

He thought he could see the disappointment in Nancy's eyes. "But I wouldn't be happy," he continued. "And if I'm not happy, what kind of father would I be?"

Nancy nodded understandingly. "So you're staying?"

"For a while," Peter replied. "I'm going to take some extra credits next semester so I can transfer to a university closer to home. I've found a single room across campus. I can't work in Thayer. And I'm going to get more involved in

Ben's life. I want to go home every weekend I can."

Nancy tried to smile but couldn't. It was as if she knew what was coming. "And Anna?"

Peter shook his head. "We're good friends. But that's it."

"Ben's a lucky little boy," she said, "to have two parents who care so much."

Peter smiled weakly. "Now comes the hard part."

"You don't need to say it," Nancy said stoically. "It's a bad time to be involved with someone else right now."

Peter just looked at her. "I'm afraid of falling in love with you, Nancy," he said. "If I keep seeing you, I know I will. But I can't. There's too much going on in my life that I need to sort out."

As Peter was speaking, he regretted every word that came out of his mouth. He realized that Nancy Drew might have been the love of his life, but a past mistake and present circumstances stood between them. Their stars were crossed—probably for good.

Nancy didn't say anything. She didn't need to. Her eyes said it all. She touched the back of his hand and planted a soft kiss on his cheek.

"What's going on in there?" Jake called as he came back in. "I hear mushy utterances."

Nancy and Peter let out relieved laughter. Jake appeared in the cubicle's opening. Peter stood and put his arm around him. "I guess I have some explaining to do."

Jake smiled. "Well, it's about time."

As Peter led Jake away, Nancy called out, "Don't be a stranger!"

Peter peeked back over his shoulder and smiled sadly. He nodded, but he knew it was over—before it had had a chance to begin. He'd always be a stranger to her.

CHAPTER 14

Bess was sitting Indian style on her floor in a puddle of papers and books, her hair a light blond pile atop her head. She was still wearing the gym shorts and halter top she'd fallen asleep in.

Professor Ross was giving a makeup exam on Monday. Though she was pretty sure she'd done well the first time, she was determined to do even better. The second she'd opened her eyes, she'd decided that this whole episode was a sign that she should shape up and be a better student from now on.

Glancing down at the papers surrounding her, she was glad she hadn't told anybody about her resolution.

"Where are you?" she queried the piles of notes, already forgetting what she was looking for. Something about respiration? Or was that the nervous system?

Across the room, Leslie raised her head from under her down comforter. Bess could feel her icy gaze. In the past, she'd cower and apologize for whatever it was she was doing that bothered Leslie. But this time she just shrugged. "Oh, Leslie. Did I wake you?"

Leslie was working her mouth as if she wanted to say something but dropped her head to her pillow with a sigh instead.

By the time Bess had returned to her room the night before after celebrating with Nancy and George, Leslie was already in bed. But people up and down the halls were talking excitedly about Stuart O'Brien, and Bess knew that Leslie must have heard.

"So," Bess said blithely, picking through her notes, "funny thing about Stuart O'Brien, huh?"

Leslie snorted.

"Whoever would have thought." Bess shook her head. "Boy, Ginny must be relieved, don't you think?"

Bess smiled to herself in the answering silence. She hated to be so mean, but Leslie deserved it. And for the first time in three weeks, she felt sure of herself in Leslie's presence. No more cowering or apologies. Maybe this is the beginning of a new relationship, Bess hoped. And Leslie will treat me with some respect.

As Leslie climbed out of bed, Bess didn't give her a glance.

"Do you have to study in the middle of the room?" Leslie sniped.

Bess acted surprised. "But—"

Leslie glowered at her. "But what? Don't I have a right to study here, too?"

"S-sure, Leslie," Bess stammered, feeling herself shrinking in Leslie's presence. "But just so you know, Ginny's coming over later to help me with some studying."

Bess thought she saw Leslie falter. "Ginny?"

Bess nodded, a slow smile lifting the corners of her lips. "Yeah. Oh, by the way, Professor Ross has offered to give her job back—with extra responsibilities."

Bess watched Leslie closely for a reaction, but Leslie only tossed her head. "Well," she spat out, "I hope she doesn't think this mess is *my* fault—"

"To be honest—" Bess began to say.

Leslie cut her off neatly. "After all, she did bring suspicion on herself. I can't see how she could possibly blame anyone else. Make sure you clean up after yourselves when you're done studying."

The door slammed, and Bess listened to Leslie's footsteps trudge down the hall toward the showers.

She shook her head. "Why did I think things would be different?" she muttered. "The human steamroller's back in business—just like old times."

"I love you," Will said as George flew toward him.

"I love you more," George replied, collapsing

171

in his arms. And she meant it. Wrapped like a present in his strong arms, she pressed her nose against his chest and sniffed.

"What are you doing?" Will laughed, holding her at arm's length.

"Memorizing you," George replied lovingly.

"But I'm not going anywhere."

"It's for later. When I go home or go to class or anywhere I have to go without you."

Will sat heavily on his bed and sighed. He ran his fingers through his dark hair. "I'm sure glad this cheating thing's over," he said, relieved.

George plopped down beside him. "It was our first test," she said thoughtfully.

Will looked at her. "What do you mean?"

"It could have easily made us mad at each other. Nancy is my friend, Andy is yours. But I feel like it's only made us stronger. I love you more now than I did two days ago."

Will threw his head back in laughter. George was beaming at him.

"What is it?" Will asked.

George laughed. "It's so great! I have to pinch myself to believe this is really me!"

"It's not you," Will said seriously. "It's *us.*"

"Forever?" George whispered.

Will nodded and held her hands. "Our trip next week is just the beginning of our lives."

An electric twinge of nervousness ran through George's limbs as she thought of their plans for their trip. She was excited. George looked into

Will's eyes. He was visibly moved, as if he knew what she was just thinking.

"Knock, knock!" someone called through the door.

Reluctantly, George and Will parted.

George ran for the door. "Andy!" she cried.

Andy dropped a long blue nylon bag in her arms and left a dozen metal stakes balancing under her chin. "There," he said, slipping by her, giving Will a wink. "Your new home away from home."

"Thanks for the tent," Will replied.

"Anything for a couple of people who just saved my life—and never doubted me."

"Did you see them moving Stuart's things out of the building?" Will asked.

Andy shook his head. "I still don't believe it. That guy's lucky he's been expelled. I wouldn't mind a few minutes alone with him."

He patted the tent. "More importantly now," he said, only half jokingly, "you guys have fun." Grinning, Andy left the room.

"We will," Will called.

George looked at Will, dropping the whole load—tent, poles, and all—and returned to his arms.

"I'm really happy for you, Dad," Nancy said into the phone, staring out her window.

Across the room, Kara threw her a questioning look. She was wearing a bathrobe and a towel piled atop her head like a swami. Nancy mouthed the words "My dad has a new girlfriend."

Kara gave her two thumbs-up. Nancy smiled, but her feelings were mixed.

"I think it's wonderful that you're seeing someone new," Nancy went on. "And Avery is a beautiful name. I'm sure she's as beautiful as her name. Yeah, I think next weekend will be wonderful. It feels like years since I've seen you."

As her father went on a little more about his new girlfriend, Nancy noticed something in her father's voice, something he wasn't saying, that made Nancy think that he might be in love with Avery.

"Oh, listen, Dad. I'm really going to have to get a computer. The computer lab here is a drag to work in, and I think it's time I joined the technological revolution. What? Really, Dad? One in your office you were going to get rid of anyway? Great! Can you bring it next weekend? That would be awesome! Thanks!"

The second Nancy put down the phone, Kara waved her over. "What do you think?" She held up a slinky outfit. Kara pulled off the towel and shook out her hair. "I have a date tonight."

"Oh," Nancy said, eyeing the array of makeup containers strewn over Kara's dresser. "I couldn't guess."

There was a soft knock at the door, then a face peered in through the crack. "Hi, Nancy."

Nancy turned her head and found Dawn standing in the doorway. Her eyes were puffy, her cheeks streaked with dried tears.

Nancy looked at Kara apologetically.

Kara held up her hands. "Wait, don't tell me. Okay, I've got to put my makeup on anyway." She slipped out of the room.

"Want to sit down?" Nancy offered.

Dawn merely leaned against the wall.

Nancy twisted the end of her shirt. She tried to put herself in Dawn's position, and decided that she'd be really angry. "I'm really sorry," Nancy began.

But Dawn cut her off. "Don't be."

"You mean you're not mad at me?"

Dawn tried to smile. "How could I be? Anybody would like Peter. Anybody would even love him. I just got off the phone with him. He told me the news."

Nancy sat heavily in her chair.

"I guess neither of us is good for him now," Nancy said. "He has a family to take care of."

Dawn nodded and finally took a seat next to Nancy. "I just wanted to come by and let you know that as much as this whole thing hurts, we're still friends." She held out her hand.

Nancy smiled broadly. "I knew there was a reason I liked you. Okay."

"How about some breakfast?" Dawn suggested.

Nancy laughed. "I can't even remember the last time I ate. I think it was yesterday morning."

"Well, you've been kind of busy. Reva was just

telling me how you guys caught that Stuart guy. You did a really good job clearing Ginny. You're a good friend, Nancy Drew, to all of us."

"Okay people, take five!"

Out of breath, Bess collapsed beside Brian on the apron of the stage. Only another hour left of rehearsal, then they were unleashed.

"You psyched to be my date tonight at the Underground?" Bess asked, leaning on Brian's sweaty shoulder.

Brian smiled sweetly. "I thought I'd bring Chris, too. Is that okay?"

"Ooh, a man for each arm!" Bess jested. "How are things going with you two, anyway?"

Brian gazed off into the darkened back of the theater. "He's great, but I'm still iffy about making our relationship so public, you know?"

"I see your point." Bess nodded. She wished she knew what to suggest. She felt closer to Brian every day, and whenever he wanted to talk, she was ready to listen. But she never knew what to say.

Bess smiled at him. "I'm really happy we can talk like this," she said. "I mean, I love Nancy and George. They're the best friends I have in the world. But you're like the brother I never had. You're like family to me."

Bess was about to give him a hug when she heard someone humming a familiar tune behind her. She gulped and froze. The Kappa anthem!

She opened one eye. It was only Casey, grinning mischievously. "Thanks, Case. You're a pal."

"Are you going to sing for us again tonight, Bess?"

"Only if you help," Bess shot back.

Casey scrambled over, leaned her head in, and hummed. Then Bess joined in, and they sang in harmony: "Oh, Kappa . . ."

Brian leaned in and joined them for the second line: "Sisterhood across the land . . ."

Pretty soon half the musical cast was laughing and singing the Kappa anthem. Bess was laughing so hard her sides were about to split!

Brian slowly climbed the steps to his floor. His knees and ankles ached. The rehearsals were starting to take a toll.

The dorm was quiet. Almost everyone else was out partying. Since rehearsal an hour ago, he'd been wandering around campus, thinking things through.

Reaching his floor, he remembered the time. "Bess!" he cried, and sprinted down the hall toward his room. He had to meet her in an hour, and he hadn't even showered!

As he fumbled with his key outside his door, Brian's eyes snagged on a folded piece of paper sticking half under his door. He knelt, and as he unfolded it, his face went white as a sheet. There was a message scrawled in pathological zigzags:

Dear Brian—Who knows you're gay? I know.
And soon, so will the rest of the world. Even
your father. Bye-bye—for now. We'll chat
soon.

Brian's hands shook violently. He looked right
and left down the hall, but it was deserted. He
balled up the piece of paper, then mashed it between his palms, beating it until it was no bigger
than a marble.

Finally he was inside, alone and safe. He threw
the paper in the garbage and stared at it. Then
he heaped other garbage on top of it, so he
wouldn't have to see it.

"Who would do this to me?" he asked the
empty room. "Who would be this cruel?"

"Nancy, over here!"

Nancy craned her neck to see over the sea
of heads. The Underground was standing room
only. A low cloud of smoke blanketed the
jammed cocktail tables, and with the candles
and the Christmas lights strung along the ceiling, Nancy felt as though she was in another
world, a small music club in New York or Paris.
Definitely not in a café on the Wilder campus.

The air was electric with anticipation. In the
last week, word about how good the Beat Poets
were had spread like wildfire. Nancy was here to
hear Ray's music, and celebrate Ginny's freedom
with the rest of the gang.

Nancy weaved through the crowd. Her

friends were all packed tightly around two cocktail tables at the foot of the stage, discussing Ginny's new acquisition: a black leather bomber's jacket.

"You look so tough!" Will exclaimed, jabbing at Ginny's arm.

"I like it," Nancy said enthusiastically.

"Me, too," George threw in.

Reva and Andy were nodding in agreement.

Stephanie rolled her eyes. "*I* think it looks dumb," she said.

"You would," Reva shot back good-naturedly.

Ginny was hiding her eyes. "Are we finished talking about me yet?" she asked.

"Almost," Nancy said, leaning across the table toward her. "I think Stephanie's just jealous. It looks awesome, and she knows it. Whose idea was it?"

Ginny smiled proudly. "Ray's. I told him earlier this week that I really wanted one. And today, he presented me with this."

George beamed at Will. "Isn't that romantic?"

"Oh no, not again!" Andy put his hands on his hips, like a school teacher: "Do I need to separate you two?"

"Try it," Nancy teased. "At your own risk . . ." She spotted Ray off to the side of the stage and held her breath.

"Ladies and gentlemen," someone announced. "The Beat Poets!"

The place erupted. Ray and his three band members swept on stage in black jeans and black

179

T-shirts. Ray picked up his guitar and began to play. The drums kicked in, then the bass. They sounded great. Their lyrics were poetic, and the music stirring.

Everyone's right, Nancy thought to herself. They *are* going to be big.

Ginny was mesmerized, watching Ray's every move.

"You can breathe now!" Stephanie screamed at her over the music, and the table cracked up.

Ray raised his hand, and the band stopped. He put down his guitar, and, shielding his eyes from the hot lights, stepped off the stage and waded into the crowd. He found Ginny and held out his hand. Ginny must have known what was coming, because she smiled at everyone and followed Ray back up on stage.

The crowd started cheering. Ray said into the mike in his gravelly voice, "This song is called 'Trust.' I wrote the music for it. This is Ginny. She wrote the lyrics." The crowd applauded again.

Ray began to sing and play, as she stared meaningfully at Ginny. It was a lulling love duet, and the words spoke straight to Nancy. She thought of Peter and of Ned, feeling a little sad.

When Ginny and Ray finished, the applause was deafening. As Nancy clapped, she saw a familiar face out of the corner of her eye, pushing toward the front. She smiled as she recognized the old blue jeans with the pen in one pocket and the notebook in the other, and the black cowboy boots. Just the sight of him cheered her up.

He hadn't seen her yet, but Nancy felt herself smiling. "Jake," she said, chuckling. "What a great surprise. Tonight's going to be a lot of fun!"

NEXT IN NANCY DREW ON CAMPUS™:

Everyone at Wilder is talking choices and changes, and Nancy's the one doing the listening. George has just come back from a camping trip with Will, and she's got some major news. Architecture student Liz Bader has a new studymate, Daniel Frederick, and they're drawing some very special designs. But Nancy needs time—to make choices and changes of her own. At *Wilder Times* she's working on a story about a frat prank that got way out of hand, and she wants to get at the truth without getting anyone hurt. And speaking of *Wilder Times*, fellow reporter Jake Collins is giving Nancy plenty to think about. The problem is, she can't be sure if the guy is good news or bad news . . . or just a passing feature in her life . . . in *Secret Rules*, Nancy Drew on Campus #5.